H

# WINTER RANGE

**Center Point**
**Large Print**

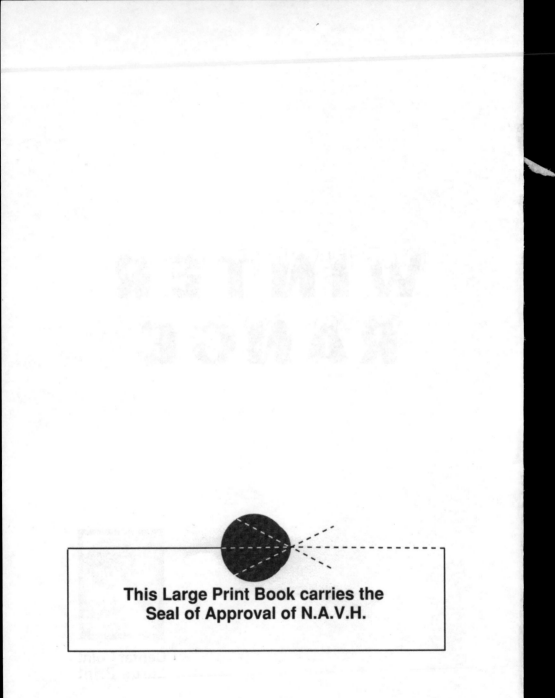

**This Large Print Book carries the
Seal of Approval of N.A.V.H.**

# ALAN LeMAY

# WINTER RANGE

CENTER POINT PUBLISHING
THORNDIKE, MAINE

This Center Point Large Print edition
is published in the year 2003 by arrangement with
Golden West Literary Agency.

The text of this Large Print edition is unabridged. In other
aspects, this book may vary from the original edition. Printed in
Thailand. Set in 16-point Times New Roman type by
Bill Coskrey and Gary Socquet.

ISBN 1-58547-277-8

Library of Congress Cataloging-in-Publication Data.

Le May, Alan, 1899-1964.
    Winter range / Alan Le May.--Center Point large print ed.
    p. cm.
    ISBN 1-58547-277-8 (lib. bdg. : alk. paper)
    1. Large type books. I. Title.

PS3523.E513 W56 2003
813'.52--dc21

2002031495

# WINTER RANGE

# CHAPTER ONE

Kentucky Jones, independent livestock trader, plunger in cattle, whirled his light roadster into the main street of the little cow town of Waterman. The car skidded in the white ruts; he recovered it, and picked himself a parking place between a cowhorse and a Ford. The same wet snow that had fallen intermittently for three days was plastered on his windshield like mashed potatoes; but he jerked his broad black hat over one eye and peered through the clear segment his windshield wiper had made.

Waterman was very full of people, for a Tuesday afternoon. Generally at this time of year the Wolf Bench cowmen were only to be found far scattered among the white-faces that perpetually lost themselves in the overpowering raggednesses of the rimrock, or haying winter-weakened cows in the long pole corrals. Today, though, either side of the street was lined with cars for three blocks; and between the automobiles stood saddled horses, dejected in the wet downpress of the snow.

Wolf Bench was not home range to Kentucky Jones; but six months in the rimrock had acquainted him with most of its people. And now from where he sat he was able to recognize many a pony that had brought its rider a heavy eighteen, twenty-odd, even thirty miles through the raw smother. He swore under his breath. Those weary, frostbacked horses meant defiance of certain of the back country roads which the snow had made impassable to cars. To get here he had himself driven all night; but the half-understood circumstances which had brought him took on magnitude, and new dark aspects, at this evidence that the whole rimrock gave it a like importance.

He turned up his sheepskin collar and stepped out into the snow, a tall, leanly lazy figure, his ordinarily humorous face relaxed in an unaccustomed gravity. It was a rocky face, made irregular by the uneven line of a nose that had been broken; but no one in the rimrock had ever seen it so austerely somber as it was now, as he turned into the restaurant known to all cowboys as the Greasy Spoon.

As he entered, however, his face lightened somewhat. He kissed the girl at the counter absentmindedly, and helped himself to a wedge of pie. "Where's the inquest going to be?" he asked.

"They're having it in the hall over Kerry's Store. It started nearly half an hour ago. They—"

"Good Lord!" He hurriedly pushed the pie wedge into the girl's hands. "Save this." He took to the street again at the trot.

Kerry's Store itself was approximately closed, but, by the huddled group which clustered under the wooden awning, he knew that the hall above was already full to overflowing. Here, upstairs, inquest was being held over the body of John Mason.

It was hard to believe that John Mason was dead, his name had so long represented unassailable strength in the Wolf Bench rimrock. That he was head of the Waterman bank had been an index but not the key to his significance. He had been a cowman once; and up to the very end he had thought as a cowman, never losing touch with the farthest corners of the Wolf Bench range. He had been in the saddle on one of his long circuits of the range in the hour that he died. His uncommon understanding of both cows and money had made him more than the kingpin of Wolf Bench finance; almost he was the economic structure itself.

Through the hard times which low beef prices had brought to Wolf Bench, Mason had managed to carry along many a weakened outfit where a nervous banker, or one less a cattleman, would have abandoned all hope. But with Mason dead the bank swayed precariously, teetering on the edge of a smash that might carry down with it half the outfits of the Bench. To many it seemed that only another Mason could avert disaster—and there was no other.

This was the man whose inquest jammed the little hall above Kerry's Store until the overflow filled the stairway, and left a milling bunch of the less aggressive in the street.

Some of those at the foot of the stair spoke to Kentucky Jones as he came up.

"Inquest got any place?" he asked.

"Been running about twenty minutes," someone told him. "They're pushing it along pretty fast—judging by what word works down the stairs. Campo Ragland's been on already. He didn't know anything new."

"Jean Ragland testified yet?"

"Uh huh. She just said that her and her father was away."

"Thanks." Kentucky moved upward, exchanging monosyllables here and there as he wormed his way

9

toward the room above. Waterman's hall was not a big one; the air was hot and stuffy here, and alive with that smothered unrest that goes with many people close together, no matter how still they sit. Ordinarily you could ride the rim for days without meeting a dozen men; and now there was a sense of impact, of smothering weight, in the sight of this place so packed, bulging with people.

He forced his way through the thick press, and finally stood looking over the heads of row on row of seated men to where a little cleared space afforded slight insulation for the dignity of the court. At a plain table sat Sheriff Floyd Hopper, looking bedeviled; at the end of the table sat the coroner, who was also the sheriff's brother. But equally conspicuous to the eye of Kentucky Jones were the faces of some of those who stood in a packed half circle around that table and behind it. Here was Clive Pierson, the banker who must step into Mason's shoes; his face was an unwholesome grey, and a muscle in the side of his face kept twitching, for in the last three days he had hardly slept. Near him was Bob Elliot, who had gambled the future of his cow outfit upon the backing which Mason would have given him, but which he could no longer expect.

And here was Ted Baylor of the Running M, and the owners of the Lazy Deuce, and the Circle Five, and the J Z—men who could cut a thousand beef steers from their herds at a week's notice, but might easily be set back to their beginnings if Mason's death should cause the bank to close its doors; and many others. Their faces were inexpressive, as they listened to this hash-over of the thing that had happened to them; but their vigilant concern conveyed itself to Kentucky Jones, making him listen intently like the rest.

Lee Bishop, the blocky, almost burly foreman of the Bar Hook, was in the witness chair, very red in the face from public speaking and the heat. Bishop was only telling what he knew about a happening which everyone had already accepted as an accident, irremediable, over with; but his nervous phrases fell upon the thick silence of complete attention.

"I was going out to the pump house, carrying a couple of pails of hot water from the kitchen," he was saying. "I aimed to thaw out the pump. Then I seen this hump in the snow—thought maybe a calf had drifted in and fell down. I went over and looked; and it was him."

"It was who?" said the sheriff cantankerously.

"Old Ironsides—I mean, John Mason."

"How long did you think he had been dead?"

"He wasn't lying there around one o'clock, when we left the home ranch. And there wasn't any snow under him. It begun snowing around two o'clock, out there."

"Then you figure Mason had this accident between one and two o'clock?"

"That ain't what I said."

"What did you say?"

"I only said there wasn't no snow under him."

Sheriff Floyd Hopper exhibited annoyance. "Let's not quibble over words! What we want is to get done here."

"Well," Lee Bishop went on with an unnecessary air of stubbornness, "I turned him over, and I saw that he'd been shot. His gun was in his hand—that long-barreled

.45 he always carried to take a pop at a coyote with, if he should see a coyote."

"Is this the gun?" said the sheriff's brother, turning toward a cluttered window ledge at one side. A deputy handed the coroner the required weapon. There was a stir all over the room as people instinctively craned their necks to see the trivial steel mechanism which, by a fluke, had perhaps kicked away the under-pinnings of Wolf Bench cattle.

Bishop identified the weapon. "Well," he went on, "I sent up a long yell but nobody answered; and I took out and run for the house . . ."

Kentucky Jones had been searching all the room for a sight of Jean Ragland, and now he was surprised to discover her so near the focus of interest that he had missed her by searching too far away. She was sitting beside her father, the big stoopshouldered owner of the Bar Hook. The two sat almost under the window ledge where a deputy kept his eye upon a muddled collection of exhibits; and the many who stood about her had partly hidden her.

Her hands were folded in her lap, and she sat with her eyes down, not looking at the crowd; but he noticed instantly how pale she seemed, so that her hair looked darker than usual against her face. If it had been possible for him to fail to recognize her he would have failed now, she looked so much smaller and more frail than he last remembered her. Had she been a stranger his glance might have passed her unnoticing, so little of her usual vividness was apparent. Then a deputy shifted his position, blocking her profile from Kentucky's view.

12

The sheriff was bombarding Lee Bishop with questions of little point. "Is that cut-off trail between the 88 and the Bar Hook often used?"

"Almighty little!" It was the first emphasis Bishop had used.

"Hooray!" said a thick voice in the back of the room; and there was a momentary scuffling sound as some of the cowboys subdued a drunken companion.

Disregarding this disturbance, Kentucky's eyes sought Jean Ragland again. Suddenly he perceived that she had leaned back so that she could peer between the standing deputies and was looking directly at him. Her eyes, which he knew were blue, now appeared startlingly dark to him in the pale oval of her face, and he found the unmistakable selectivity of her gaze mildly surprising, so that he shifted upon his feet. He smiled at her; but her face did not change.

Then suddenly he was aware that she had signaled to him, secretly beckoned him to draw nearer. It had been the faintest narrowing of an eye, the slightest inclination of her head; yet he knew absolutely, as she again averted her face, that a signal had been conveyed.

Deeply puzzled, he began to work his way along the side of the hall. The sheriff, he noticed, was perspiringly pushing ahead with his questions, evidently very conscious of his far-gathered audience. The sheriff's brother, the coroner, was nudging him, but he was barging ahead, as Kentucky Jones presently reached a point not more than three yards from Jean Ragland. He was still separated from her by the thicker press of men which had been forced back from around the coroner's table; but here he stuck.

He was trying to catch Jean Ragland's eye as the sound of scuffling and contention broke forth again in the back of the room. The sheriff glared, faltered, and stopped. A tall deputy left Jean Ragland's side to go pushing back through the crowd.

Watching the disturbance at the back, Kentucky Jones did not see that Jean Ragland had left her chair until she stumbled almost against him. Her handkerchief was at her mouth, and she seemed even paler than before, as if turned suddenly faint by the stifle of the close air. Campo Ragland, her father, sprang up and was beside her in a stride, supporting her in his arms. For a moment the press of the crowd was too much and they could not get through. Her shoulder pressed hard against Kentucky, but although he spoke to her by name she did not appear to hear.

Then unexpectedly, in the smother of the crowd, her fingers closed upon his in a quick, hard grip. She had pressed a small heavy object into his hand.

Turning it over in the pocket of his coat, Kentucky Jones discovered with a queer slow stir of the blood that the thing she had left in his hand could be nothing else but a used bullet. He knew at once that this was the slug which had killed a man.

Campo Ragland said through his teeth, "Will you let us out, or not?" and the standing cattlemen flattened against the wall to let Campo and his daughter by. Kentucky Jones lost sight of Jean as the crowd closed behind them.

But for Kentucky Jones the atmosphere of that packed

room had changed. He was no longer simply a cattleman interested in a death which threatened to shift the economics of a range. The thing that had pulled him over four hundred miles of snow-clogged ruts in the last eighteen hours suddenly took on a new aspect, as acutely personal and definitely sinister as if he had himself been accused of murdering the man who was dead.

And now the inevitable sequel broke. A deputy who had stood by the cluttered ledge where the exhibits were sung out sharply, interrupted the sheriff.

"Wait a minute! Hold everything! There's something missing here!"

In the momentary silence a lower voice said, "Maybe it's fell on the floor." There was a shifting of feet and chairs as a couple of the deputies stooped to hunt about among boots and chair legs.

"What is it?" the coroner demanded. "What's gone?"

"This here bullet's gone, that we had on the window sill with the other things!"

"Bullet? What bullet? You mean—"

"The slug that killed Mason!"

There was a sudden moment of struck silence all over the crowded room. This was followed immediately by a rising buzz, as almost every man of all the great numbers in that room turned to speak lowtoned to his neighbor. The sound swelled stronger and stronger, becoming a drone like that of swarming bees—the irrepressible and somehow menacing sound of a crowd which has instantly comprehended the significance of what has passed.

Watching the stir about the coroner's table, Kentucky

saw that Bob Elliot, owner of the 88, was looking at him curiously. Kentucky grinned faintly at Elliot as he worked a hole in the seam of his pocket with a thumbnail, and pressed the bullet through, so that it fell deep in the lining of his coat.

Over the buzz of confusion he heard the coroner almost shouting, "You sure it was there?"

"It's been here all the time, but just now I reached back, and—"

The sheriff jumped to his feet, and his chair clattered over backward. His voice rose in an angry bellow. "Lock that door," he ordered. "By God, I'm not going to have it!" An abrupt silence fell at the impact of his voice. "Some of you fellows are no better than children. I suppose you'd steal the shirt off your own back if you figured it was a souvenir! I—"

"Wait a minute, Floyd." The coroner caught the sheriff's arm, and pulled him down to whisper in his ear; and there followed an inaudible but apparently a heated discussion. It seemed to take effect upon the sheriff's plans, for he sat down abruptly, his square face flushed with exasperation. "All right, let it go, for now. But somebody hasn't heard the last of this! . . . Go ahead and give 'em cause of death."

Kentucky Jones drew a deep breath. He had come up into this crowded room to attend a routine hearing, calculated to confirm the death of a man who, however important to these people, had only died foolishly, accidentally, by his own gun. But now the inquest as such had lost all meaning, turning into a sham, an apparently unconscious fraud.

16

A sudden incomprehensible anger overshadowed reason as he wondered if Campo Ragland knew that the bullet which killed Mason was not what it seemed—and had prompted his daughter to get it out of the sheriff's possession. If her theft of this scrap of evidence was not in behalf of her father, then who? If Jean Ragland was being used by her father or anyone else as a cat's-paw in a dangerous situation, he meant to find it out. Once more he worked his way sidewise through the crowd along the side of the room, this time toward the exit.

## CHAPTER TWO

Campo Ragland had taken his daughter to Waterman's rambling one-story hotel, and had returned to the street again by the time Kentucky Jones, after a fifteen-minute search through Waterman, again located the boss of the Bar Hook.

Kentucky strolled up, greeting Ragland with the slow singularly infectious grin that served him as a passport through hard times and slack, wherever he went. That grin had friends from the Pecos to the Madres. Campo Ragland, grim as was his mood, half smiled in return as they shook hands.

"Seems like people didn't hardly realize how important Mason was around here, until now he's dead," Kentucky began. "Of course, he naturally had enemies."

"You can't run a bank right," said Ragland lifelessly, "without raising up an enemy here and there." The boss of the Bar Hook was not quite as tall as Kentucky Jones, perhaps because of the over-accentuated bow of his legs; but his lean, stooped shoulders were very broad. His eyes were blue, like his daughter's but deep-set in sun-squinted lines. And though the general aspect of his face was benign, as if forty-odd years of wind-driven dust and snow had rounded its harsh corners and edges, it was a face which could set grimly and stubbornly, turning into a fighting face.

"Curious," said Kentucky Jones, watching Ragland closely, "that everybody was so ready to accept that he went to work and shot himself—accidentally."

"What else could it have been but accidentally?" Ragland said impatiently.

"Nothing, I guess," said Kentucky; "but on pretty near any other range somebody would most likely have tried to prove there was a shenanigan."

For a moment Campo Ragland's eyes turned upon Kentucky. Watching him intently, Kentucky Jones could not, however, see that the man's face changed. "I suppose so," said Ragland, without expression; and he half turned, as if he would walk on.

Kentucky Jones wavered an instant. His cautious prodding had failed; but its failure was more challenging than a revealing answer. He plunged.

"Mr. Ragland," he said, "can you use a man?"

Ragland's eyes quickened. "I don't want no more of these flivver tourists we get for cow hands today. But if you got in mind some good steady—"

"I was speaking for myself," said Kentucky Jones.

"Come off! You're a cattle trader."

"Times are bad, Mr. Ragland; the more so with Mason dead. I was a brush popper before I was a trader, and I'm a good one yet. And I'd sure like to fill in at it for a while."

The owner of the Bar Hook rubbed the salt of red stubble on his chin with a gloved knuckle and stared at Kentucky, obviously puzzled. "Of course you realize," he said, "what I want is just a plain cow hand—not no advisory board."

"Plain cow walloping is all I want," Kentucky assured him.

"Well," said Ragland doubtfully, "if you want a plain riding job for the rest of the winter, at fifty-five and found, I sure can't refuse you; though I must say, it comes as a kind of surprise."

"I'm on then," said Kentucky.

"You'll have to take a horse, the way the roads is. I'll leave an order at the livery barn you're to have a Bar Hook horse. . . ."

The inquest was over as Kentucky Jones returned to Kerry's Store. Some who had made the journey by horse were already mounting ponies which moved out reluctantly, head down against the plod which many would not finish until long after dark. Kentucky Jones joined one of the big groups which talked it over on the sidewalk.

"Verdict come out same as expected?"

"Oh, sure; 'Accidental discharge of his own weapon.' The jury didn't hold off more than a minute and a half. Say! The sheriff wants to see you."

"Where is he?"

"He went along about ten minutes ago."

"All right."

Kentucky Jones moved off down the street in unhurried long strides. As he reached the sheriff's little frame office Floyd Hopper was in the act of leaving, having just ejected, with diplomacy, more worried cattlemen than the little structure could comfortably hold. For Kentucky Jones, however, he reopened his door.

"That you, Kentucky? I thought you headed south to see about some feed contracts, or something?"

"I did, but I headed back, when I heard."

"Come in here, Jones." Hopper jerked a ragged window blind downward over the door's glass pane and flung himself into a chair. He produced bottle and glasses. "We run this all the way from below the border," he said blandly.

"See you got your inquest over."

The sheriff puffed out his cheeks and blew an exhausted blast. "Damnation! Can you beat this? In the whole Wolf Bench country, here was just one man that couldn't be done without—one man that as good as held the rimrock cattle in the hollow of his hand—and a rabbit jumps, and blooey! He's gone. Great guns, Kentucky! Any other man, any other time—"

Kentucky Jones waited, studying him. There is a certain type of man who seems fated to pursue public office, somehow perversely unfitted for anything else. Hopper was such a man. His straight-clipped grey mustache, his flat loose-skinned jowls and full-fleshed eyes somehow unmistakably advertised the public office holder—not incompetent, but definitely limited.

"Any other man could have been spared better," he raved. "Even John could have been spared any other time. But with Wolf Bench cattle on the ragged edge of

20

bankruptcy, and the lowest beef prices since—"

"Does Clive Pierson—he steps into Mason's shoes, doesn't he?—does he know anything about cattle?"

"A little, and maybe a little about banking. But with Mason dead all confidence has collapsed. Yesterday and this morning there was a crowd in front of the bank to see if it would open its doors! Clive Pierson is scared stiff—ready to stampede any direction. Some think already that he'll break half the outfits on Wolf Bench, and the bank too, if he can save the outfits he's got his money in. No man knows where his brand gets off. Nobody trusts his neighbor. Wolf Bench is in a shape where you touch a match to it, it'll go up like a celluloid collar!"

"Maybe it'll adjust," Kentucky offered.

The sheriff burst out at him with something very like fury. "Adjust? It'll adjust like a dogie calf to a wolf! This throws the whole damn range out of balance! And you stand there and tell me—" He paused hopelessly, out of words. "There you have it." He lifted his hands and let them fall with a gesture of morose futility. "This is a good sample of the raw edge of temper the whole rim-rock is on. I call you up here to ask you a favor, and in two minutes we're jumping down each other's throats."

"That's all right," said Kentucky. "If disorderly conduct was my field, I expect I might be feeling somewhat ants-in-the-undershirt myself."

"Disorderly conduct is right," the sheriff said. "Man, you'll see plenty now! Half the range is sore at the other half already. Take the Circle Five and the Lazy Deuce. Or the Three Bar and the Running M; today them two owners met face to face and never spoke. Or take—"

"Take Bob Elliot's 88 and Campo Ragland's Bar Hook," Kentucky prompted.

"There you are—maybe the worst case of all. Those outfits have always jangled. And now look at it! Elliot don't own a fifth of his range. The rest is leased Indian land. Now Elliot's lease is out. Them leases have to be bid for—and everybody knows that there's more than one big outfit will never let that lease go cheap. Elliot depended on Mason to let him take the money for his bid. Now it's all over the range already that the bank won't back him. Elliot can't get any quick price for all that landless stock; he's through."

"He laid himself wide open for this," said Kentucky. "He's blown the 88 up to three times its natural size— like a balloon."

"What if he did? Now that he busts, is he supposed to like it?"

"And what about Ragland?"

"Ragland's Bar Hook could probably stand through the storm, if it wasn't for the misfortune to Elliot. But Ragland's open range is the open range nearest to Elliot. What if Elliot turns and floods his cattle onto the Bar Hook graze?"

Jones already knew that the Bar Hook was at least half on public domain. By the cowman's code Campo was entitled to the use of that range because he had developed water upon it; but he had no legal hold upon the unfenced.*

*Only about 50% of the land in New Mexico and 17% of the land in Arizona is privately owned (1925). Of Nevada's 550,000 cattle, 85% are on open range.

"Are you convinced in your own mind," Kentucky asked him, "that Elliot will dare shove his herds onto the Bar Hook range?"

"I know this," said Floyd Hopper, heavily, somberly. "Elliot don't need more than four or five riders to take care of his winter work. Yet he's laying on extra hands. He's hired on at least six more men just in the last couple of days, since the death of Mason. You know how it looks to me? Like he's not waiting for the day he'll have to move. Like he's not even going to wait the winter out before he starts filtering into the Bar Hook range."

"In that case," said Kentucky, "Bob Elliot is sure a man who enjoys to grab a bear by the tail and go round and round. Campo Ragland will fight like a whang-doodle in defense of its first born."

"Sure, they'll fight. They'll fight to a standstill. I'll have a full fledged cattle war on my hands within the month! And what can I do about it? Nothing, by God! Off in the hills somewhere three or four cowboys meet three or four others, and start trading private opinions. Then—wham! The guns come out, and one, or two, or three go down. No one bears witness, no one lodges a complaint—there's just those good boys dead, and that's all."

The sheriff was glaring as if he were already looking through gun smoke. "Suppose I make a guess who forced the fight, and slap somebody in the calaboose? Before night half the range is raising hell to get him out. The preliminary hearing throws out the case—and I've lost five hundred votes. And two days later there's another killing somewhere else!"

"I know," said Kentucky. "Hell afloat and no blotters."

The sheriff grunted. Suddenly a new grievance seemed to occur to him, and the explosiveness came back into his voice again. "I'd give a hundred dollars to lay hands on the son of a gun who swiped that bullet out of the inquest. Right out from under my damn nose, by God!"

"Well," said Kentucky, "lead's cheap; it wasn't worth much."

Sheriff Hopper savagely pulled off his hat and slammed it on the edge of his desk; it fell unnoticed to the floor. "It'll do 'em no good," he declared. "It isn't as if we didn't have the—" He stopped.

"The other bullet?" Kentucky asked.

The sheriff seemed to go relaxed and cold, all of an instant. He studied Kentucky with a questioning eye. "Why did you say that?" he said at last.

"Well," Kentucky apologized, "you were just remarking you had something on hand that would take the missing bullet's place."

The sheriff's steady stare did not drift from Kentucky's face. "We took a mold," he said at last. "We took a mold of this bullet, that's gone."

"That was a smart thing to do," said Kentucky.

"I expect," said the sheriff. He dropped his eyes, and his hands fidgeted with the miscellany on his desk. "Just the same," he said, returning his eyes to Kentucky's face in a cold and smoky gaze, "that was a very strange question, Mister, for you to ask. I had a hound dog once, that got in trouble that way."

"Trouble, sheriff?"

"By sight running."

24

They looked at each other, two men who had said more than rested upon the surface of their words—one of them unwillingly. Kentucky Jones began rolling a leisurely cigarette; and he grinned, the slow infectious grin that could make a dog follow him, or a woman remember him, or could make a man forget why he had meant to paste him a couple.

Sheriff Hopper stirred restively, and dropped his eyes. "I was just thinking of something," the sheriff said.

"What was that?"

"You're a sight runner," said the sheriff again; "but I don't know but what you're a good one. Sometimes there's a use for a feller like that. And that was what I wanted to see you for. That was a good job of scouting you did for the Cattle Association last year; and I—"

"Who told you I ever did any 'scouting,' as you call it, for the Cattlemen's Association?"

"Old Man Coffee told me, up-country in the Frying Pan."

"Sometimes Old Man Coffee gets too damn eloquent," said Kentucky Jones, exasperated.

"Well, anyway," said the sheriff, "I was hoping I'd find you kind of at loose ends around here; like as if you might be able to take and do something different from what you'd figured to do."

"As for instance?"

The sheriff fidgeted. "There's an end hanging loose in this Mason case," he admitted finally.

"So? I thought it was all decided that Mason committed suicide by mistake?"

Hopper made an annoyed gesture. "The case is closed.

John Mason died of the accidental discharge of his own gun—that's established. But it just happens that there's a man has come in with a perjury."

He paused. "Yes?" said Kentucky Jones after a moment. "To what effect?"

"Well—we questioned him about Mason's death; and later I found out he wasn't where he said he was."

"You sure you want to tell me this?"

"I'm not telling you anything that ties you to anything—yet. Now, this feller—maybe he was in sight when Mason got killed. Or maybe in earshot. Anyway, he lied about where he was—tried to make a fool of us, by God! And I mean to hook him for it."

"Hardly seems important," Kentucky said speculatively, "if there's no question about how Mason died."

"It isn't that," said the sheriff gloomily. "There's some awful bad times ahead of us here, Kentucky; and we got to show that the law has teeth in it while we still can. Now, if you don't mind taking the time, there's a thing you could do for me that would be an almighty favor."

"Come to cases," said Kentucky.

"This man I'm telling you about is out at the Bar Hook. Now I realize you're a cattle trader; but oftentimes a feller like you will take a riding job to fill in with, over the winter, or something—especially in times like this. Now if you'll go to Campo Ragland and get a job, you can find out about this feller for me in a way that I couldn't myself, nor the deputies neither."

"You want me to hire on at the Bar Hook and root this feller out for you—is that it?"

"That's the idea."

Kentucky Jones was looking out the window, down the snowy street. Half a block down, in front of the hotel, Jean Ragland's pony stood. Her father's horse was elsewhere—down at the livery barn most likely, for Campo Ragland would be sitting about on oat bins, hashing over the inquest with cattlemen of his own particular faction. It would be Jean, and not her father, whose initiative would get the Bar Hook horses started on the homeward trail. Now, watching from the sheriff's window, he saw her come out of the hotel, untie, and mount.

He had seen this girl but half a dozen times in his life; yet she had singled him out today to aid her in a thing which he did not yet fully understand. She had been surrounded by friends, by men she had known all her life; even her own father had been there. Yet, for some obscure reason she had turned to him. He watched her now as she brought the little black pony up the street at a running walk.

Jean Ragland sat her pony with the easy lax grace of young muscles raised in the saddle. Now that she was in her own element again she no longer looked frail and small, as she had in the crush of the inquest, but competent and at home on her horse, as he had known her before. As she passed she looked straight at the window where he stood, and Kentucky believed that she saw him there.

Floyd Hopper smoked morosely in the shadows brought by the closing of the early dusk. "If you want to go out to the Bar Hook for me, I can make it worth your while. What we got to do is—"

"I wouldn't touch it with a ten foot pole."

Floyd Hopper stared at him irritably. "Just because you're gone on Campo Ragland's girl doesn't have anything to do with this job. This is for the protection of the Bar Hook people, as much as anything else."

"Protection or no protection," Kentucky Jones said shortly, "I won't touch it. As far as Campo Ragland's girl is concerned, I'll tell you straight and plain that if Mason hadn't been killed within fifty yards of her door, I wouldn't be here now."

"I guessed that," said the sheriff drily.

"You guessed it, and now you know it; and beyond that—to hell with you!"

Floyd Hopper made a disgusted gesture. "And right. I don't blame you much. It's pretty near too much to ask a man, to step square into the makings of a range war that's none of your own. I guess you're smart to stay out of it, all right. I only wish I was—"

"I'm not out of it," said Kentucky Jones.

The other looked up at him, startled.

"I've already talked to Campo Ragland," said Kentucky. "He's given me a riding job. I'm going out and ride for the Bar Hook until this thing clears up."

The sheriff said, annoyed, "You just said you—"

"Hopper," said Kentucky Jones, "how long have you known that John Mason was murdered?"

It took a moment or two for the sheriff to convince himself that he had correctly heard; but when it had soaked in he came to his feet with a jerk. His eyes flared narrowly, but his face was grim and tight. "You accusing me of lying at the inquest?"

"Yes," Kentucky Jones said.

Floyd Hopper's leathery face turned a deep maroon, and in the shadows his eyes seemed like points of light. "Then," he said, "it's because you know a lot that I don't."

Kentucky Jones grinned faintly, re-lit his cigarette, and shook his head.

The sheriff's voice was heavy and intent. "Come out with it, Jones! What's your play here?"

"I'm going to try to get me the man that killed Mason."

They stared at each other. "Jones," said the sheriff, "let's get this straight here. Are you working with me or not?"

"Not," Kentucky answered.

The dark color of the sheriff's face, which had faded slightly, now deepened again. "You look here, Jones! If the time ever comes when it can be shown that Mason was murdered—and the man who murdered him can be turned up—"

"Maybe that time," said Kentucky, "is coming quicker than you think."

"When it does come, I'll make my play, and I'll make it stick. In the meantime—think twice, you, before you buck me! You can make plenty trouble if you want; I've got no doubt of that. But it's you that'll burn if you do!"

"Reassure yourself," Kentucky told him. "If I can't make a finish play, I'll make no play at all."

"I don't know," said the sheriff, "but what you'll go a little farther than that if you know what's good for you."

"You mean—?"

The sheriff's voice was low, but his words had more force than if he had thundered. "I mean you'll sit out of this altogether."

"I told you what I'm going to do," Kentucky said shortly. He was in a hurry now to be on his way; he wanted to hit the Bar Hook road before the final closing of the dark.

The sheriff shouted at him, "You infernal—"

The door came open, shuddering as it broke clear from the ice that had formed at the sill.

## CHAPTER THREE

The man who now stamped the snow off his boots upon the threshold was straight-backed and lean-shouldered; his age was indeterminate—he might have been forty, or he might have been much more. He had a clean-cut, knife-carved face, set with blue eyes as clear and penetrating as sharp bits of ice. And he radiated a driving, thrusting energy, so definite as to convey an almost physical sense of impact.

Floyd Hopper said without warmth, "Hello, Elliot"; and Kentucky Jones said, "Howdy, Bob."

Kentucky Jones had always been on good terms with Bob Elliot before; but now Elliot looked over the other with a coolly noncommittal eye. "I heard," Bob Elliot said, "you got yourself a job today?"

"That's so."

"Bar Hook?"

"Yes."

The boss of the 88 looked Kentucky over again slowly, with a certain bleak irony. Then abruptly he turned away, breaking into the painful-sounding cachinnations which passed with him for laughter. You might not have recognized that laughter as such, at first, even if you had known Bob Elliot for some time, for he was not known for any outstanding hilarity. It consisted of a shaking of the shoulders and a series of coughing sounds, accompanied by a general pained, cracked-up look, but no expression of enjoyment. While this went on he always turned away from his companions as if the unaccustomed onslaught in truth seized him against his will.

The paroxysm died away. "And with a face like that," Bob Elliot was able to say at last. "Oh, naturally! Oh, of course!"

"I've found it a useful face for fighting a wolf," Kentucky agreed equably. "Still, I don't see——"

"Just the brand," said Bob Elliot, "that always goes loco over the nearest gimlet-headed girl."

There was quiet while a man could count fifteen. "I'm going to finish rolling this cigarette," said Kentucky Jones, "and I'm going to roll it right. Then I'm going to see if I still feel the same way about that last remark. And if I do—I'm going to smash your teeth down your throat."

"Maybe you are," said Bob Elliot, without emotion. "Floyd, I hear somebody rustled the bullet that killed John Mason."

"Uh huh," said Hopper.

"I'm not sure that I saw that done, Floyd," said Elliot, disregarding Kentucky now, "but I think maybe I did; and I think so more and more."

Sheriff Floyd Hopper came awake. "Who was it?"

"I don't want to name a name," said Bob Elliot. "unless we can make a test to see if I'm right. If I'm right, the party that took that bullet passed it on to another; and I don't think this second one passed it on. I don't know but what he's just dumb enough to have it still."

"And where is it?" said the sheriff.

"I think," Bob Elliot said, "that you'll find the bullet in the clothes of this man here: Kentucky Jones."

The three were motionless for a moment. The sheriff stared from one of them to the other. "Look here—"

"That settles it," said Kentucky. He smashed Bob Elliot across the face with his open hand.

The owner of the 88 staggered against the wall, spun half around with the weight of that openhanded slap. His face went white, his lower lip curled downward, and through the exposed teeth his breath sucked in.

Jones said, "Take care of yourself." Elliot's hand made a whipping snatch at the gun at his right thigh as Kentucky struck again, this time with his closed left hand. Elliot's head snapped back; he seemed to teeter for a moment, face upward, then buckled at the knees and went to the floor like a dropped saddle blanket.

"For God's sake get out of here," said the sheriff. "Get out of this town! He'll kill you when he comes up. . . ."

Campo Ragland struck a match, and as the light of three or four lamps filled the room the faces of the riders likewise lightened. They had been more than four hours on the way. From Waterman, Kentucky Jones had pushed his horse steadily, and as darkness closed down he had overtaken the Bar Hook people. With them he had ridden the long Bar Hook horse trail across the Bench, until they came out at last upon long rolling reaches, and the rambling buildings of the Bar Hook loomed before them, dark and shapeless.

The kitchen wing in which they now gathered was built of big square-hewn logs; but the interior was neatly plastered, roomy, and hospitable, like the kitchens of the big Spanish-grant ranches a long way to the south. They could cook for the combined outfits of Wolf Bench in that kitchen, when need arose.

Jean Ragland said, "There's no fire made." And Kentucky noticed the odd way in which they all fell silent for a moment, as if it was a strange and uncommon thing that a fire should not spring into being and set coffee on itself, at a deserted ranch.

"You see," Campo Ragland said to Kentucky, "we generally have a cook around here; lately it's been a lame boy named Zack Sanders. Used to be a rider, but his horse fell on him and turned him into a cook." The broad bland curve of his forehead receded to thinning hair the color of rust. Where his hat protected his forehead it was blotched with freckles, suggesting what a bran-spattered face he had offered the world in his youth. "But this boy is kind of gone missing on us, it seems."

"Been missing long?"

"Last week he was supposed to take two days off, and he rode over to see a girl he has over here thirty, forty miles," Ragland said. "I didn't notice it so much Saturday, when he didn't come in, that being the day that this—this accident happened to Mason. But in Waterman today his girl said he left there Saturday sun-up. That's four days gone."

"He'll probably show up," Lee Bishop grunted.

"Oh, I suppose so." Campo Ragland jerked himself into activity again, and began throwing wood into the great stove. "The way things have been going around here, it gets a feller nervous, I guess."

In a little while the big stove began to fill the room with a lazy warmth, and the hot smoky smell of frying beef and potatoes began to thaw the riders out. Kentucky Jones, a butcher's apron draped over his easy-going frame, whistled through his teeth as he dug out caches of canned goods with the unerring instinct of the born grub-hunter. With the heartening warmth the mood of the Bar Hook changed, so that for a little while it could have been any ranch house, anywhere—except that the presence of Jean Ragland made a difference here. That girl could subtly change the time and place, making it different from any other ranch house and any other night. Perhaps no cowboy ever rode for the Bar Hook without feeling that he was in some part riding for this girl.

Looking at her now Kentucky Jones would not have guessed that she had today testified concerning a death that had occurred within fifty yards of this door; and that in the midst of those proceedings she had felt impelled to thieve the heart out of the evidence of that death. The cool balanced poise of her head and the quiet of her face—beautifully alive even in repose—belied the shadow which he knew must hang over her here like a storm cloud over a lonely rider trying to hold his herd.

He had come here to find out the exact nature of the shadow which had fastened itself on the Bar Hook, and upon Jean Ragland as a part of the Bar Hook; and, accordingly, he turned now to studying the others as they ate. Lee Bishop, the solid, square set foreman, was not a man, he decided, who could be counted on for any very great variety of imagination nor quickness of insight. Undoubtedly he would stand steady as a rock in a pinch. Evidently he was a man born at a branding and raised in the saddle, for he would hardly have attained a foremanship at thirty had he been handicapped in experience.

The other two cowboys Kentucky Jones classified as a couple of kids. Jim Humphreys, though only five years younger than Bishop, would perhaps always be a kid. And Billy Petersen was the youngster, essential to every outfit, who would be given the undesirable jobs of horse-wrangling and night herd, and errands which were a nuisance. Two more cowboys who had been reluctant to leave town were expected in before morning; and when these were in, the winter outfit of the Bar Hook would be complete. The outfit as a whole was typical, ordinary.

But Campo Ragland remained silent throughout the meal; and for the moment Kentucky could make out no more about him than he already knew—which was little enough.

"Sure miss Zack Sanders around here," Campo said at last, getting up. "Might's well set out what we'll need, handy to breakfast, I guess."

"Dad," said Jean, "I'll take care of all that."

"You get along to bed," her father told her gruffly. "I want you to get some sleep."

Jean hesitated, as if she would argue the point; but appeared to reconsider, and obediently picked up a lamp.

Kentucky Jones moved efficiently about making ready for morning, bringing wood handy to the stove, locating the breakfast grub, as if preparing against an intricate problem. Out in lonely camps upon the range these men would have got their own breakfasts effortlessly, without thought; but here, where a cook was supposed to be, a cookless breakfast loomed as an ordeal untold.

"I wish I knew—" Campo began; he was ladling fresh coffee into a big pot with an enormous spoon—"I wish I knew—" Suddenly he stopped, and stood staring, while from the poised spoon a thin trickle of dry coffee dribbled to the floor.

Jean Ragland had returned, and was standing in the broad doorway. She still carried the lamp, and its sharp near light, illuminating her face remorselessly, showed that her features were drawn by a hard and unaccustomed emotion. It took a moment or two for Kentucky Jones to realize that what he saw in the girl's face was fear.

For a moment no one spoke. Jim Humphreys let an armload of wood fall with a thundering crash. Then Ragland said, very low, his coffee spoon still motionless, "What is it, Jean?"

Jean Ragland's voice could hardly be heard. "Someone's been through the house."

"Been through the house?"

"Ransacked it—through and through!"

Her father let the big spoon splash into the coffee pot. Jean turned, throwing the light into the room beyond, and for a moment father and daughter stood together in the doorway, staring at what the others could not see. Then slowly, with a curious uncertainty, Campo Ragland moved out of their sight. Jean followed him with the lamp.

Billy Petersen, the youngster, made a jump for his sheepskin coat, jerked a gun out of its pocket, and stuck it in his waistband; Jim Humphreys said, "Don't be a damn fool, Billy!" And they followed Kentucky Jones to the door through which Campo had disappeared.

The room which Kentucky Jones now studied from the doorway was long and broad, but it had the low log-beamed ceiling common to the northern ranches, rather than to the desert layouts of the southwest. In one end a huge fireplace with a six-foot opening was built of rugged chunks of the native rock, and near this Campo stood, holding up a second lamp. The owner of the Bar Hook was turning slowly, his face expressionless as he combed the details of the room.

They heard him say, "You're right; there's no question about it."

Jim Humphreys said, "Is there anything we can—"

Ragland shot them a quick glance, as if momentarily he had forgotten that he was not alone. "It's nothing much, I guess," he said in a rocky voice. "This dump has been searched, all right. That's all. Wait back, you."

Jim Humphreys and Billy Petersen returned to the kitchen. At the doorway Kentucky Jones turned and stood for a moment in a final survey of the main room.

He saw Ragland pass on into the next room. Jean moved to follow him.

Then suddenly the girl stopped and stood rigid. Following her eye, Kentucky Jones saw at once what she was looking at. It was a trivial thing; yet sufficiently out of the way to identify itself at a glance as the focus of the girl's attention.

On the wall hung a cheap picture frame, perhaps ten inches in its longer dimension, made of narrow dark wood, with acorns represented at the corners. And it was distinguished from other picture frames by the fact that there was no picture in it. Through its glass could be seen the torn manila paper which had backed the frame, and a section of the wall.

Jean Ragland set her lamp down, stepped forward and jerked the empty frame from the wall. For a moment she stood irresolute, glancing quickly about her.

"Do you want me to wrangle that for you, too?" said Kentucky from the doorway.

For an instant she stared at him, her eyes wide and hostile. It was surprising to him—a little. That afternoon, at the inquest, she had pressed into his keeping the bullet she had taken from the evidence. But now he knew that she had not elected him as her ally, nor wanted more than momentary aid.

Her father's step sounded close at hand beyond the other door. Jean dropped the picture frame behind a wooden chest that stood against the wall, and picked up her lamp again as her father re-entered.

They went back into the kitchen. Billy Petersen, Jim Humphreys, and Lee Bishop were waiting there, as they had been told to wait. Campo Ragland paused in the main room a moment to exchange the briefest sort of word with Jean. But his announcement was to all of them, at once.

"Somebody's ransacked this dump," he told them slowly. "Somebody's ransacked it good. There's a rifle gone."

Lee Bishop said, "Is that all?"

"They pried open the cash box, but didn't take anything, so far as I know. It beats me."

"We can spare a rifle, I guess," Jean said sharply. Except for a certain soberness, Kentucky was unable to make out in Jean's face any sign of the cold still terror he had seen in it a little while before. But he saw now that a change had come over Campo Ragland. Campo's face was stiffly expressionless; his eyes those of a man lost in uncertainty.

Kentucky Jones did not know Campo Ragland well. In the course of his efforts to establish himself in rimrock cattle, he had held parley with Campo perhaps half a dozen times. But he knew Campo to be typical of the Wolf Bench breed of owners, a man as durable as the hide of his own range-bred ponies. Behind his genial façade Campo had always been completely sure of himself. But now, while the outer aspect of the man was still little changed, Jones saw that the inner confidence was gone, as if the qualities which had made him the fit boss of a hard-held and forever-resistant range were cut through at the root.

"We may as well get some shut-eye, I guess," Campo said. "One of you fellers better turn out in the morning and load the stove."

"I'm a pot-buster," Kentucky offered. "Leave breakfast to me."

"All right. Might's well turn into Zack's bunk, then."

Alone in the little lean-to room off the kitchen where Zack had lived, Kentucky Jones sat for a little while on the bunk, and smoked a final cigarette. The bullet that Jean had taken from the inquest was now displaced in his mind by the empty picture frame which the panic-stricken girl had hidden from her father's sight—and his puzzlement was immeasurably increased. It was time to take stock of what he knew.

He did not conceal from himself that his interest in the murder of Mason turned upon the involvement of Jean. The foundation of the thing was, of course, the fact that John Mason was dead, shot from the saddle within fifty yards of Ragland's door as he arrived from the 88 on Bob Elliot's pinto horse. Jean Ragland had stolen from the evidence the bullet that had killed Mason—and the sheriff probably had the mate to that bullet. Upon this foundation now rested a miscellany of puzzling and unrelated detail.

A Bar Hook rider had lied about his whereabouts at the hour of Mason's death. A lame cowboy cook was missing from the Bar Hook. Somebody had ransacked the Bar Hook ranch house, taking away a rifle and a picture out of the frame. Jean thought little of the disappearance of the rifle, much of the empty frame. Unquestionably, he needed more of the missing fragments before he could piece that picture together.

In the meantime the range was thrown out of balance

by the death of the cow financier. Bob Elliot, facing ruin, could save himself only by forcing Ragland over the edge in his place. In one stride Kentucky Jones had stepped into a situation of greater pressure than any he had before encountered in an active life. Things had happened at the Bar Hook which did not explain themselves, and other things would follow upon them which, could they be foreseen, must be averted at all costs.

For what seemed a long time he lay awake, listening to the snap of the frost in the heavy timbers of the house, while his mind quartered the case like a lion hound failed of the scent. Presently he became aware that there was something he had left undone. Without striking a light he opened a seam in the lining of his coat and extracted the bullet which Jean Ragland had pressed into his hand that afternoon. He opened the window, and found that the snow was drifted here against the log wall. Kentucky Jones hesitated a moment more; then flicked the bullet that had killed John Mason out into the drifted snow.

## CHAPTER FOUR

Whatever else happened the work had to go on. Campo Ragland had contracted to ship five carloads of long two-year-old steers to a southern feeder, but although the cars were already waiting on the Waterman siding, the gather and cut for the shipment still lacked many head. The two other Bar Hook cowboys—Harry Wilson and Joe St. Marie—had come in from Waterman during the night; and with his full force Campo himself jumped into the job of finishing the work in a day.

After breakfast Kentucky Jones made an opportunity to familiarize himself with the scene of Mason's death. "I suppose," he asked Lee Bishop, "that's the pump house?"

"Yeah, that stone dump. The place where I found Mason is about three horse-jumps southwest. He was lying face down with his head this way, and I—but I guess you heard all that. The trail he was coming in off of, from the 88, strikes four mile down the edge of the cut and then turns along the edge of the rim, and strikes the 88 layout after about eight mile more. There's a shorter way up over Cat Ridge; but what with the rocky going, it takes about as long."

"It worked out so I missed part of the inquest," Kentucky said. "Did it come out why Mason was riding from the 88 to the Bar Hook? Seems kind of funny—the way things stand between the two brands."

"Yeah, that was all thrashed out," said Lee Bishop. "Old Ironsides was always a great hand to keep in touch with all corners of Wolf Bench; and he was just making one of his regular circuits of the range."

"I heard he was riding one of Elliot's plugs."

"Yeah. His way of doing was to borrow some horse that could be counted on to go home by itself, and at the next outfit borrow another such a horse, and so on. This time he was riding an 88 horse."

"Yes, I got that," Kentucky said. "One of Bob Elliot's top horses—a big pinto, with white forelegs."

"So they said. We got to get going, Kentuck. You and me aren't working with Campo today; there's a little job over here we got to wrangle separate. Rope you a low grade horse."

Kentucky had expected that Jean Ragland would make a chance to talk to him; but Lee Bishop was in a hurry to be on the move, and they took the trail toward the rim before Kentucky could talk to Jean alone.

For a long time they rode in silence; Bishop had given no hint as to the nature of their errand, as yet.

"I don't know exactly what we're up against here," the foreman said at last; "I haven't said much to the old man yet. I think we'll be able to tell just about how it's going to work out when we get up here four, five mile. It's made a beginning, I think."

"What has?" said Kentucky.

"You'll pretty soon see. I wish to God Jean was out of here. There's no better cattle woman anywhere than Jean. But this might not be a good place for her, pretty quick here."

"What's become of her mother?" Kentucky asked him. "Seems like there used to be a Mrs. Ragland, last summer when I first came to Wolf Bench."

"There's still a Mrs. Ragland. She's putting in the winter out on the coast."

"I reckon she's got judgment," said Kentucky. "I hear that out there they've got a big rock candy mountain, where the rivers are whisky, and the cows have rubber horns. Though, come to think of it, that might not interest her."

The foreman shrugged moodily. "You can call it judgment. It looks more like a run-out, to me." He checked himself, already sorry for what he had said. He tried to apologize, and made it worse. "There isn't anybody

43

means any better than Mrs. Ragland does; it's just that somehow she doesn't take to cattle, I guess."

"Looks like Jean would have gone with her?"

"Jean takes after her father," Lee Bishop said. "This busted-up country is bred into her blood and bone. She's a true Ragland. There's been a Ragland running cattle on Wolf Bench since the first long-horn showed."

"And how long has there been an Elliot?"

"Well, there's always been an Elliot too; though until Bob Elliot took it over from his old man, the 88 was just a kind of a chicken-yard outfit. It's Bob that's got ambitious."

Kentucky Jones decided to try one of his shots in the dark. "Lee," he said casually, "have you let anyone in on the fact that Mason was not killed at the time he was supposed to be?"

Lee Bishop did not respond for a moment; then he turned to face Kentucky Jones slowly. "How's that?" he said without expression.

"Let it go," said Jones.

"Kentucky," said Lee Bishop, "I want to know what you were driving at."

"Not much, Lee. From the way you talked at the inquest, it seemed to me like you didn't join in with the others in figuring that Mason was killed before the snow begun."

"I said," Lee Bishop responded combatively, "that there wasn't no snow under him, didn't I?"

"You mean you grant that he was dead before snow flew?"

The foreman did not answer for almost a hundred

paces. Then he burst out with a sudden unaccustomed display of black temper. "I'm tired of these here everlasting questions! I don't want to hash this thing over no more, you hear me?"

They came out now upon a high point of the rim, a monstrous declivity so sheer that it seemed as if at some time the world itself must have cracked to let the desert down. Far below the Bake Pan country began, a flat plain stretching into blue distance. Only here, from the heights, did a man get a full view of that vast flatness. Perhaps it was just as well that a rider out in the middle of that illimitable desert land could only see a little of it at a time. Seeing it all at once any horseman would have had a right to be disheartened; just as a man who could see his whole life ahead of him might not have the heart to go on.

At a glance the vast flats of the Bake Pan seemed utterly devoid of life. Cowmen's eyes, however, could pick out here and there among the dark dots of sage and catclaw other dots that were cattle. They grazed in little scattered bunches, and the bunches themselves were far between, for this land could carry but ten or fifteen head to the mile. But what interested the riders on the rim was something else—a greater concentration of cattle, a long, dark irregular string of them lying on the face of the desert like a blacksnake whip.

"Uh huh," said Lee Bishop. "There you have it! How many head would you count that drive?"

"Maybe twelve hundred," said Kentucky. "88 stock?"

"Sure they're 88! You know now why Bob Elliot put on six more hands!"

Already, then, this thing had come. Legally the public domain was open to all, whatever tradition or moral justice might hold. But Bob Elliot must have known that the brand which held this range would defend it bitterly; and this land had been Bar Hook graze for a long time.

Perhaps, Kentucky Jones considered, Bob Elliot could not wholly be blamed. It was hard to withhold all sympathy from a man making a stubborn fight in the face of a crush-out. But it seemed to him that there was something grossly unnatural about the manner in which the move was being made. The force of Elliot's motive, as well as his general method, he could understand. In Elliot's position almost any enemy of Ragland might have been expected to attempt a gradual infiltration of the Bar Hook range. But this sudden, openly-hostile mass move was like nothing Kentucky Jones had ever seen. The thing was too swift, too unequivocal, too bald-faced.

"Eight riders," Lee Bishop commented. "He certainly is figuring to make this stick! He wouldn't be laying on all those riders if this was anything more than a beginning, Kentuck."

"Can the Bar Hook stand it, Lee?"

"We'll damn well see," said Lee Bishop. He squinted at the sun. "It's pretty near a three-hour ride to get down to where them cattle is, but I guess we got to go; sorry we didn't bring no sow bosom and hard-tack, Kentuck."

"To hell with grub," said Kentucky, swinging his horse into the down trail.

It was warmer down on the Bake Pan, and the snow which lay deep and unbroken on Wolf Bench had here already dwindled to wetly glistening rifts. Across the long flat reaches the cattle plugged dustlessly, to a persistent bellowing of cows separated from their calves. Out from the herd, as the Bar Hook men drew near, rode a lank angular man on a hammer-headed roan pony.

"This is Bill McCord," Lee Bishop said in an undertone; "he's from away. Bob Elliot's run through half a dozen range bosses in the last three years, but this one will suit him, I guess. He—"

"Yeah—I know him. If he found you drinking at a crick he'd ride through upstream, to see if you objected to mud. Hello, McCord."

McCord ignored Jones. "Howdy, Bishop."

"I see you're moving a few head of stock," Bishop began.

"Figure to," said McCord. The two foremen eyed each other. A certain amount of humor showed in the hard-seamed lines of McCord's face, but it was the kind of humor that starts trouble; and in his green eyes there was no humor at all.

"Moving right on through, I see," said Bishop.

"Some day, maybe," said McCord. "Not this year."

"No?"

"No," said McCord, his voice casual. "Wouldn't be surprised if we'd stop and turn free, up here ten mile."

"No," said Bishop. His voice too was casual, as if he were answering a question. "No, these cattle aren't going to stop and scatter up here ten mile. Not anywheres near it."

"You don't mean to tell me?" said McCord. "Why, I heard this was open range."

"Open," said Bishop, "from your nearest water half way over to our nearest water; and not one calf jump more!"

Two cowboys had left the loafing cattle and were walking their horses toward the parley with a studied detachment. McCord now signaled them with a motion of his head, and they came up to range themselves a little behind the 88 foreman. Both were armed; but Kentucky recognized neither.

"So?" McCord said to Bishop.

"So," said Bishop. "I'm right sorry to have to set you right on these few mistakes. We'll spare you feed when we've got feed to spare. But just now the Bar Hook bunches are working down off the Bench. There'll be another four thousand head on this range, right soon."

McCord grinned, his eyes unwavering from those of Lee Bishop. "I ain't interested," he concluded dispassionately. "I got my orders—and I'm carrying 'em out."

Kentucky stirred uneasily in his saddle, sorry to see that Lee Bishop was getting mad.

"Save yourself trouble," Bishop was saying. "This herd is going back into the grave it belongs in; and it's going deep back, son!"

The half grin suddenly dropped from Bill McCord's face, and in its place flashed an ill temper exceeding Bishop's own. He kicked a spur into his horse so that it spun and brought up with the right side of horse and man toward the Bar Hook riders. This move brought squarely into view the holstered forty-five that swung behind Bill McCord's right thigh, below his short coat. Until now the 88 foreman had kept his right hand in his pocket; but he now brought it to the reins beside his left, and they saw that his right hand was ungloved.

"Why, my short friend—" said Bill McCord, his voice hard and even; and he began to swear, slowly and distinctly, his green eyes ugly on Bishop's face. The cursing of Bill McCord was neither varied nor picturesque, but it was hard-bitten, personal, and direct, and its slow evil-toned syllables carried enough efficient ugliness to raise welts on the hide of a mule.

"Put your scabby pony up that rim," Bill McCord finished; "go tell your old man that I put your proper name to you, and sent you home!"

For a moment no one spoke. The foreman of the Bar Hook sat his horse like a frozen man, apparently unable to believe his ears, so unexpected, so unaccountably sudden had been the break. Then the blood rushed to Bishop's head. With a wrench of his bit he put his horse staggering against Kentucky's; the animal danced crazily, mouth high and open to the raw jerk of the curb. Bishop thrust a widespread shaking hand at Kentucky. "Gun," he stuttered. "For God's sake—give me gun—"

"I haven't got any gun, Lee."

For an instant Bishop hesitated, rigid in the saddle, his horse dancing under him. Then an inarticulate curse broke in his throat; he slashed the spurs into his pony and it bounded forward at the horse of Bill McCord.

Kentucky swung himself half out of the saddle in a wild snatch at Lee Bishop's rein, and managed to catch it near the bit. As the pony whipped to its haunches, Kentucky struck Bishop a terrific wallop on the back with his open hand, seized his foreman's shoulder, and shook him hard.

"Hold it, Lee—damn it, you hear me?"

Abruptly Lee Bishop quieted, straightened in his saddle, ran his gloved hand uncertainly over his eyes. The color was draining out of his face again, leaving it grey. For a moment the man had been insane.

"I'll take it," Lee Bishop said at last.

"And you'll like it," said Bill McCord.

"I'll take it, and I'll like it," said Bishop, his eyes expressionless on McCord's face. "Enjoy it, you! Because you'll never see the like of it again."

Bishop turned his horse, unhurrying, no longer rigid in the saddle, and walked his pony away.

Kentucky followed; but as he turned he saw that there was no satisfaction in Bill McCord's grin. Rather it seemed to him that the man was disappointed, chagrined.

Suddenly he thought he understood McCord's deliberate attempt. For some definite reason that remained unknown, Bill McCord had done all he could to make an opportunity to kill Lee Bishop—in self defense.

The climb to the rim was a laborious one, and the early dusk was no more than an hour away when they again reached the home ranch of the Bar Hook. They were nearly in before Lee Bishop had anything to say.

"I haven't carried a gun," he declared, "since I was a kid, except to hunt with; and I never pulled a gun on a man in my life. But if I'd had so much as a bean shooter— I'd have killed McCord where he sat."

"Tell me one thing," Kentucky said. "What in all hell did you figure to do there when you jumped your horse at him?"

"I don't know," Bishop admitted. "Seems like my thinking machinery slipped out of gear."

"Do you know any reason why McCord should want your scalp?"

"That's just what gets me," Lee Bishop said. "Doggone it, I hardly know the man. He knew I had to tell him to move his cattle back."

Kentucky tried a new shot in the dark. "Lee, how long have you known that Bill McCord was mixed up in the killing of Mason?"

Bishop stared at him. "What you talking about, boy?"

"That man has some reason for wanting to down you, Lee. Ask yourself what you know that isn't good for him."

Bishop did not answer for nearly a quarter of a mile. "It beats me, Kentucky; I can't think of anything I got on him. If I'd only had a gun—"

Immediately they sought out Campo Ragland, whom they found moodily swallowing scalding coffee in the kitchen, his boots clogged with half-melted snow. Lee Bishop briefly told his boss of the drive of the twelve hundred head—the prompt, bold beginning of Elliot's play for the Bar Hook range. Of his own clash with McCord he made little.

"McCord cussed me out good. I would have took a poke at him, one time there, only Kentucky reached out and kind of steadied my horse."

"Twelve hundred head," Ragland considered. His eyes brooded heavily upon the coffee pot. "Well, if that's all of 'em, I suppose the range can stand it; I've seen worse years for grass."

Lee Bishop stared at him dumbfounded. "All of 'em!" he finally exclaimed. "Of course that ain't all of 'em. You'll find out that this here is only a pointer and a beginning. It's the start of a freezeout, that's what it is."

Ragland said moodily, "He's in no shape for that."

"Sure he's in no shape for it," said Lee Bishop spunkily. "But it's what he's after just the same. He's going to load that range, taking what death losses he can't get out of. His only chance of hanging on after he loses his lease is to crowd in here before then—that's what we've got here!"

"He's sure forcing his hand," Ragland growled.

"Sure he is. It's going to be one brand or the other before that boy's through."

"It's bad all right," Ragland admitted.

"Come tomorrow," Lee Bishop said, "I can take our boys and go down there and stop that herd; and—"

"Elliot isn't going to draw back his cattle. He'll—"

"Then, by God, we'll smear into them and put 'em back!"

"They'll pistol-whip you, you start that stuff!"

"I don't believe—" Lee Bishop began. Then he changed what he had started to say. "Well, then, I suppose," he said, "we'll just have to pistol-whip 'em back. Me, I don't know any other way."

Campo Ragland slammed his coffee cup onto the stove. "I don't want any of that," he said. "That's old-time stuff—it don't go nowadays. Nobody ever made anything by any such business yet."

Lee Bishop stared at him. "Maybe," he said, "I better

ride in and ask the sheriff would he please ask 'em to move back as a personal favor to him."

Campo Ragland threw his foreman a short ugly glance, but did not reply to this sarcasm directly. "After all," he said, "you got to make allowances. That brand is fighting for its life."

Lee Bishop looked at Kentucky, turned away, and hopelessly spread his hands. Kentucky led the way out; it was time to feed hay, anyway.

"What the devil's got into him?" said Bishop as soon as they were outside. "Do you suppose he's going to lay down and quit on us?"

"Maybe he's holding back to kind of catch Elliot on the rebound," said Kentucky.

"How, for instance?" demanded Lee Bishop contemptuously. "Yah! He's on his knees like a shinneried bull."

"He sure set up an over-hopeful holler," Kentucky admitted. "Does he generally bust out with the shilly-shallies this way?"

"No! I've never seen him like this before." Bishop fell into a moody silence while they walked as far as the hay racks. "Look here," he said, suddenly turning on Kentucky. "You know what's holding him back?"

"No," said Kentucky honestly.

"I know! I know only too darn well. I tell you—" His voice stopped as sharply as if he had been struck, and he stood staring past Kentucky Jones.

Spinning on his heel to follow Bishop's eyes, Kentucky saw that the foreman was staring at a forlorn dun horse which stood low-headed before the bars of one of the corrals. An arm's length of broken rein dangled from one side of its bridle, trailing on the ground; and it stood spread-legged to avoid the chafe of a saddle that was no longer on its back, but under its belly.

"So Zack is dead," said Lee Bishop slowly, at last.

"His horse?"

"Yes."

## CHAPTER FIVE

A new sense of shock and malignant uncertainty descended upon the Bar Hook people with the return of Zack Sanders' low-headed horse, Zack's broken saddle under its belly. Lee Bishop and Kentucky Jones called Campo Ragland out, and the owner of the Bar Hook examined the horse and its equipment in a black mood.

"Unsaddle him and feed oats," was all Campo said. And he returned to the house.

The other riders, as they returned from their work, had more to say. To these men Zack Sanders was no mere name. Some of them had known him for a long time, worked stock with him often before the fall of his horse had turned him into a cook. Now they were faced by the assumption that he lay dead in some unknown place, lost in the rocks and snow.

"He shouldn't have tried that trip," Jim Humphreys said. "I bet you it was his game leg made him fall."

Harry Wilson, a small man, wizened beyond his middle age by many a winter in the saddle, allowed that this was the bunk. "If that's so, how comes that streak of blood on the swell of his saddle fork?"

Billy Petersen, the young horse wrangler, said, "Maybe he was fixing to shoot a rabbit or something, and his horse shied, and as he fell the gun went off—"

The boy stopped. Probably there was no one there who had not seen immediately the parallel between this suggestion and the accepted theory of John Mason's death. Somehow the improbability that this could have happened twice threw doubt on the theory that it had happened at all. There was an awkward pause.

Jim Humphreys said he didn't see why Zack's horse hadn't come in before, if it was coming. "Here Zack's been missing since last Saturday. That's—let's see— going on five days. And here this horse don't come in—"

"Probably he tried to go back to the wild bunch, but the wild bunch kicked him out."

"How long do you suppose he's run loose?"

"It couldn't have been long or the saddle would have got lost off."

"I've heard of 'em staying on a month."

When the other riders had gone about their work of feeding the stock, Lee Bishop took Kentucky Jones aside. The blocky foreman was in a subdued but lowering temper. "It's bad when you learn that a boy you've known for a long time is dead," he said; "but it don't change the other thing, Kentuck, nor take off of us what we got to do. I don't suppose there's anything we can do for Zack Sanders now, but in the meantime Bob Elliot is swamping the Bar Hook range. Right now, while we talk, I suppose he's turning free the cattle that we saw moving onto our range today. Tomorrow they'll be getting ready to move a thousand more—and that won't be the end either. We got a fight on our hands, Kentuck, and that's the next thing here."

"Just before Zack's horse come in," Kentucky said, "you were starting to tell me what was holding Campo back. There's the kingpin of the situation, Lee—if you're right that you know what it is."

Lee Bishop's face took on the stubborn look of a man who thinks he will be disbelieved. "This may sound funny to you, Kentucky, but I've known these people here a long time—a sight longer than you have, and I know that I'm dead right."

Kentucky waited, while Bishop studied the ash of his cigarette. "Kentucky," said Lee slowly, "it's Jean Ragland that's holding her father back."

Kentucky considered this. "What makes you think so, Lee?"

"There isn't anybody in the world has any influence with him except her—not even her mother. The rest of us come and go and he pays us no more mind than horses. But Jean—she can fan him just as handy as she fans a bronc. If she makes up her mind there will be no war with Elliot, there'll be no war, and Campo will watch Elliot work his ruination, and never smoke a gun."

Kentucky Jones thought he saw the chance to probe a side trail. "Maybe," he said, "that's why he had that big picture of her hanging there in the main room."

"What big picture?"

"Don't you remember?" said Kentucky. "The picture that's always hung on the wall of the main room, right opposite the kitchen door—about so high and so wide, with the frame made out of black wood, and onions at the corners?" He was describing the position and appearance of the empty frame which had so startled Jean the night before.

"Onions at the corners?"

"Well, some kind of carved-on vegetable."

"That wasn't no picture of Jean."

"Then whose picture was it?"

"I don't know. Just some guy on a horse."

"What kind of looking horse?"

"Just a horse. What the hell do you care?"

"Nothing. It's kind of interesting to see who remembers what."

"Here we got a couple of deaths," said Lee Bishop disgustedly, "and a range fight that's about to make the Bar Hook a thing of the past, and our old man quits on us, and we're backed up against the wall—and all you can find to think about is some guy had his picture took on a horse!"

"All right," said Kentucky. He picked up the other thread. "Anybody can see Jean has a heavy drag with her father—and maybe is the only one that has. But that's slim backing, Lee, for what you said. What was your other reason"—he watched Bishop steadily—"for thinking that Jean is keeping her father from making a stand against Elliot?"

"Other reason?"

"Didn't you have another reason that you haven't given me, Lee?"

Lee Bishop hesitated for a long time. "No," he said at last.

"Lee," said Kentucky, "if Jean doesn't want her father

to scrap it out with Elliot, what do you suppose her reason is?"

"How do I know what her reason is?" said Lee Bishop explosively. "How does any man know what any woman's reason is? Maybe the trouble we've had here already has made her sick of guns, and she's afraid that if we stand our ground there'll be more of these here empty saddles come in under the bellies of horses."

"Have you talked to her, Lee?"

Lee grunted a negative, and hesitated again, groping for words. "Look here!" he burst out at last. "Look here! *You've* got to talk to her!"

"Me?"

"There's nobody around here she'll pay any attention to but you. Some way she's got a blind on the old man's eyes and she's keeping him snubbed down helpless. Kentucky, I tell you," Lee Bishop declared savagely, "if we make our stand against Elliot now, it may be we can turn him, and get out of it cheap. But the farther this thing goes the harder it will be for him to draw back. If this thing goes too far there will be no way but to fight it at a deadlock until one or the other is smashed. Most likely both will be smashed. You've got to talk to that girl!"

"What makes you think I can do anything with her, Lee?"

Lee Bishop groped for some way to express a thing that he sensed, but could not prove. "She follows you with her eyes," he said at last. "Whatever you do, if you aren't looking, she follows you with her eyes."

"Horsefeathers!" said Kentucky.

"Maybe; but you got to do what I say anyway," said Bishop stubbornly. "What chance we got here, the way things stand now? We're not going to have enough range left to keep our brand on a jackrabbit. Talk to that girl!"

"You think," said Kentucky, "there's anything about the cow situation I can tell her that she don't know?"

"You got to get her to pull out of here until this thing is over. You got to get her to go out on the coast and join her Ma, or go for a visit in Flagstaff or Cheyenne, or some place—don't make no difference where she goes. But you got to get her to get out of here and leave this thing to her old man to work out in his own way."

"I see a swell chance to get popular, with that," said Kentucky. " 'Excuse me, ma'am, kindly ma'am, would you just as leave get the hell out of the state?' "

"You'll talk to her?"

"No," said Kentucky. "Do you think I'm a damn fool?"

"Yes," said Bishop.

He lingered at the corrals, however, after Lee Bishop had ridden off to have a look at the condition of the Waterman road; and presently, as he had more than half expected, Jean Ragland came out to look at a lamed pony.

"I don't know but what we ought to fire this," she said, running a hand over the pony's swollen stifle.

"I'll rub some of them chili beans on it, that I fixed for breakfast," he told her. "And maybe I'll bind on a pad— a couple of them left over pancakes of mine will be just the ticket."

Jean straightened, dropping pretense. "I want to ask

you about a couple of things," she said.

"I was kind of looking for you to," he admitted.

Jean Ragland said, "You have the—thing I gave you?"

He regarded her gravely. "That bullet?" He told her what he had done with it. "I don't know that it did any good to get hold of it, though."

She stared at him a moment. "Do you think—"

"I don't know for sure," he said; "but I'll gamble you that the sheriff has the other bullet."

The back of her gloved fingers went to her mouth, but her face was calm, and she was not afraid to meet his eyes. "What other bullet?"

"It's possible I'm wrong. I'm not in the confidence of the sheriff—or anybody else. But I tell you for what it's worth; I'll bet my last cent that that bullet has a twin; and that the sheriff has it."

"But what makes you think there were two?"

"Well—he was cussing because the bullet had got away from him; and he said that taking it wouldn't help anybody, because even if they needed it they had the— and there he stopped. So I asked him if he meant they had another slug."

"And what did he say?"

"It kind of made him mad, and we had a little dispute. But finally he said that they had taken a cast of the bullet. Now, I took that last to be a lie."

Jean's face was troubled. "Why?" she asked sharply.

"Sometimes," he said, "you ride by a bunch of brush that looks like there ought to be a deer bedded down in it; but you look at that brush and somehow you know that there's no deer there."

60

"I see."

"The sheriff offered me a job," he said. He told her now about what Hopper had wanted him to do concerning the Bar Hook man who had not been where he had said he was when Mason died.

She nodded promptly. "Yes, I know who he means."

"I gathered that several people know about it; but not I."

"It doesn't amount to anything," she said quickly. "It was just a rider here—that quarter-blood Indian, Joe St. Marie. I'm certain he—doesn't know anything about it."

Kentucky Jones now knew St. Marie as one of the two cowboys who had come in during the night, a blunt-faced, competent rider, not so dark of skin that his Indian blood would have been conspicuous had not his flair for personal decoration in cut steel and silver work betrayed him.

"St. Marie is the best bronc rider we've ever had here," Jean said. "But he isn't always dependable. If he wasn't working where he was sent the day Mason died, that isn't the first time he's goldbricked his job."

"You don't think his perjury means anything then?"

"That's all silliness!"

"I thought it sounded that way. Of course I told Hopper I wouldn't touch his proposition with the end of my rope."

She said peculiarly, "Yet, after you talked to the sheriff, you went to my father and got this job."

"Absolutely not! I had this job before I talked to Hopper."

"Then why," she asked him bluntly, "did you want

this job?"

He considered. "Maybe," he said at last, "it was partly because it looked to me as if you needed some help in something you were trying to do."

She said slowly, "Do you mean that, Kentucky?"

"It stands."

"Then—" she spoke with difficulty—"you're free to go. Ride out of this, and try to forget everything that has happened here! Some day I hope to see you again; I swear that I truly appreciate what you've done. But there's nothing more that you can do here now."

"I'm not so sure of that," he answered.

"What can I say," she burst out, "that will make you believe me?"

"Tell me this. Who asked you to try to get that bullet out of the evidence, Miss Ragland?"

He had failed to surprise her. She looked directly at him, and the blue of her eyes appeared paler, like the color of clear ice, and as little revealing. "No one," she answered flatly. "I wanted it for a souvenir."

At this suggestion Kentucky could not suppress a chuckle. "If by any chance that were so," he told her frankly, "that would be far and away the coolest thing I ever heard of being done."

He saw her color slowly, and her gaze flickered, but she stood her ground. "You—you don't know what you're saying. But—of course you're right. It was a silly, loco thing to do; maybe the worst thing I could have done."

"And yet," he said gently, "you'd do it again."

She averted her face abruptly. "It seems like," she said,

half to him and half to herself, "I ask too much of people, way too much, always."

"You've never asked anything of me."

"I made you carry the bullet away for me."

"That doesn't count."

She turned to face him. "Then I'll ask something of you now."

"*Bueno.*"

"Taking that bullet was a fool, crazy thing to do. You say I'd do it again. That's as may be. But now I want you to forget that it ever was done. That must never be known—never in this world! Do you understand?"

"That's all right," he agreed, "as far as that is in my control."

"As far as—what do you mean?"

"I think," he said, "that somebody saw you take it."

Her lips parted but she did not speak; and she waited, watching him.

"The man that saw it isn't sure of what he saw; but he's made a sharp guess. He even suspects that you gave the bullet to me."

Her question tumbled out of her. "How do you know that?"

"He came into the sheriff's office while I was there, and he accused me of having received the bullet. He even said I probably had it with me then—which I did."

"Who?" she demanded. "Who was that?"

"Bob Elliot," he told her.

She turned from him with a queer dull swaying movement, like a little tree turned by the wind. "Oh, dear God!" she whispered. Abruptly she turned back to him.

"What did you say? What did the sheriff do?"

"What could I say? I just stepped into Elliot and cracked him down."

"You—*what?*"

"I took a smash at him. He ducked into my left, and dropped like a thrown-down rope. The sheriff—"

"Stop!" she ordered him. Turning his eyes to her he was astonished to see that her face had gone white with anger. "That was the worst thing you could possibly have done! I wish—I wish you'd never set foot on Wolf Bench!"

He said slowly, "I can't blame you for that. But—"

The intensity of her anger cut him off. "For heaven's sake, shut up! I don't want to talk to you now."

She climbed the fence, swinging over it easily, like a man.

"Wait a minute," said Kentucky; a sudden quickening of his voice arrested her. "I just now got an idea, here."

"I don't think anything you can say can interest me," she told him.

"This will interest you," he said gravely, "if I happen to be right."

He had been watching Lee Bishop ride in at a walk from the look-over he had been giving the road to Waterman. Twenty yards from the place where Kentucky Jones and Jean Ragland stood, Bishop struck a match to the cigarette he had rolled. As he raised the cupped flame to the cigarette, his horse shied with a sharp sidelong whip that put out the match, and they saw Lee Bishop's lips move as he swore.

Kentucky crawled through the fence. "That's happened ten times today," he said. "How is it, Lee, that half the ponies shy when they pass that rock?"

"Cussedness, I guess. Maybe that rock looks like a bear, to them—I dunno."

"Looks like they'd get used to it, then. Have they always done that right there?"

"Well, no, come to think of it. Say—I wonder if there's a dead coyote under that snow?"

Lee Bishop dropped to the ground, and the two walked back to the rock which conceivably, to horses' eyes, looked something like a bear. Lee Bishop explored the drift with his boot.

"Uh huh," he exclaimed, "that's just what it is!" He thrust gloved hands into the snow.

Then Bishop hesitated, stood up, and stared at Kentucky Jones blankly. The blood that had come into his face as he bent over drained away rapidly and completely, leaving his face grey, and somewhat silly of expression. "No, it isn't," he said in a curious voice.

It was Zack Sanders they found, under the drift. He had been shot twice, and had died where he fell; and they saw that he had fallen in this spot before the first of the snow.

## CHAPTER SIX

If it had been a shock to the people of the Bar Hook when Zack's horse came in, the finding of Zack's body was a bombshell in truth. Examination established definitely in the minds of them all that Zack's death could have occurred at no other time than that ascribed to the death of Mason; for the same factors which had established the time of Mason's death applied here also—tho time of snowfall, and the brief hour during which the Bar Hook had been deserted before the fall of the snow.

Campo Ragland made repeated and insistent efforts to get in touch with the sheriff by phone, but Floyd Hopper was not in Waterman, nor could he be located. Under the intense pressure of the implications carried by the unwelcome discovery, the Bar Hook people found that they had little to say to each other. More than the death of a cowboy cook was involved here. No one could any longer suggest that Mason's death was an accident. The man whose death so desperately weakened the position of rimrock cattle had been murdered—almost within the shadow of this house.

Yet, until the sheriff could be located, there seemed to be nothing that they could do that night but wait.

Kentucky turned in late, and with no great hope of sleep. The finding of Zack Sanders' body had given immediacy to a situation with which he was not yet prepared to cope. He had hoped to satisfy himself as to what had actually happened in the Mason case before the irresistible march of events brought disaster to the Bar Hook. Instead, all the rimrock would know tomorrow that the Bar Hook had been the scene, not of an accidental death, but of a murder, the result of which promised to ruin half the brands of Wolf Bench.

Once more he juggled in his mind the ill-assorted facts in his possession, trying to align them through the medium of his new knowledge.

The obvious assumption—that Zack Sanders and Mason had killed each other—he discarded at once as

66

beyond all probability. Undoubtedly this would be the sheriff's first recourse, he thought; and he decided to leave it to that official.

Yet, barring this foolishness from his calculation, he was unable to make headway toward rearrangement of what he knew. It would have been easy to suggest that Joe St. Marie, who had lied about his whereabouts at the hour of the crime, might have killed Zack Sanders as the result of some obscure quarrel and then killed Mason because Mason was a witness. This did not, however, explain Jean Ragland's theft of the bullet that killed Mason; nor her alarm over the fact that a picture had been stolen from a frame; nor her anxiety to conceal this loss from her father.

If one thing was certain it was that he knew too little about Joe St. Marie. For a little while he experimented with the extraordinary hypothesis of a love affair between St. Marie and Jean. St. Marie had killed Sanders because of a quarrel, then Mason because Mason was a witness; Jean, feeling sorry for St. Marie, had stolen the bullet to protect him; St. Marie had stolen a rifle from the house to suggest that the missing weapon was the weapon used; and while he was at it, he had stolen a picture of Jean Ragland. Here the hypothesis blew up; the picture stolen had not been a picture of Jean, but of "some guy on a horse."

Suddenly he recognized the startling folly of a solution which contended that the sensitive and somehow innately patrician daughter of Campo Ragland was infatuated with a quarter-blood rider of broncs. He swore at himself. What he knew was that Jean was inextricably involved in a murder which was a disaster to all of Wolf Bench; and that as a result of this murder the 88 herds were pouring across the Bar Hook range. For the present he had to admit that he was sure of nothing more. He closed his mind to the puzzle, and tried to drowse.

But presently he found himself roused sharply to a new wakefulness. For some moments he lay listening intently, unable to decide what was wrong. Then there came to his ears the slip of cold wood on wood. The sound was distinct, yet somehow stealthy; he knew at once that someone's hand had fumbled in an effort to take down the bars of a gate in silence.

Kentucky Jones stepped to the open window. He could not see the corral from which the sound had seemed to come; but now he heard the snow-muffled hoof beats of a walking horse, unhurried and very quiet except for the dull crunch of the snow.

The night had only a thin sliver of a moon, but a frosty clarity; against the clean sparkle of the snow all snow-less objects stood out in etched relief. Near the down-country trail a horse and rider now appeared, to disappear at once behind the stone pump house. Kentucky swore under his breath. He had been unable to recognize the rider, but the horse he knew—a tall black with a long white stocking on the off fore. It was the horse Joe St. Marie had ridden that day. Horse and rider came into his line of vision again considerably further away, and, immediately dropping behind the fall of the land, were lost to view.

Kentucky Jones returned to his blankets with his nerves on a peculiar edge. He rolled a cigarette, and thought of Joe St. Marie.

The crack bronc rider was a man of peculiarly mixed type. Almost no trace of accent or guttural came into his speech. And if the build of his head suggested the Indian by a certain breadth at the eyes, it gave him an effect of strength, as if the crossbreeding behind him had done him no great harm. St. Marie was unusual in that he made no effort to conceal the dark strain in his blood. The big steel conchos on his five-inch belt and the silver work of his spurs and bit were barbarian touches hardly ever seen in the Wolf Bench rimrock any more. Joe St. Marie must have cut a broad swath among the mestizo girls in Mexican quarters.

These things were apparent at once; and so little further insight into this man was afforded by better acquaintance that many must have supposed that this was all there was to know about Joe St. Marie. Kentucky Jones was not so sure. St. Marie was too compactly self-sufficient, he thought, to be so easily known.

He was able to fix upon one immediate probability. If Joe St. Marie had gone out, he would presently return. Had he meant to jump the range he could have used any number of subterfuges for giving himself a long start before his absence was noted. St. Marie would be back that night; and, since he had not bothered to pick a fresh horse, he probably did not mean to be long gone. Kentucky dressed, and propped himself up in the corner of his bunk to watch the pump house trail.

An hour passed; more than an hour. Looking at his watch he was astonished to learn that it was only quarter past eleven o'clock. Sometimes he had dozed, but he was certain that he would have heard St. Marie's horse if it had come in. He smoked again, and waited ten minutes more.

Upon the snow a spot appeared. It pulled up, shifted and separated, and he saw that it was not one horse but two. For a moment or two both riders sat motionless, plainly in view against the snow; and the watcher made out that the second horse appeared to be a pinto, for he could not see the animal's fore legs, and thus knew that they must be white. Suddenly he knew that he was looking at the pinto horse of Bob Elliot.

Kentucky Jones spat through his teeth, and anger rose into his head like a rising wind. Now that he had identified the horse it was as if Bob Elliot stood before him, so that he sensed again the driving, thrusting energy that swung ruination across the Bar Hook range in the form of long herds of trampling white faces.

And here for the first time was something definite and conclusive, upon which a man could lay his hands. The Bar Hook rider, whom he was now certain was Joe St. Marie, had ridden out to confer with the boss of the 88. He promised himself that within five minutes he would know exactly what that exclusive saddle conference meant.

The pinto horse now turned, going back the way it had come; and the other rider, coming on, was lost to view again in the dip of the ground.

Kentucky Jones took up the long-barreled Colt which had so seldom emerged from the bottom of his war bag, and checked its action to see that it was free of frost. Promptly he stepped through the window and ran to the corner of the house. Against the far corral stood a stable shed of peeled logs. To this he made his way, keeping it between himself and the trail. Within the long shed, across one end, was fixed a horizontal log, used as a saddle rack; he knew that the rider would return his saddle here. Beside it, in black shadow, he took his post.

It seemed to him that the night was silent for a long time before finally he heard again, close at hand, the small crunching complaint of the snow under the hoofs of a walking horse. He distinguished the creak of saddle leather as the rider swung down; and once more he heard the stealthy slip of cold wood on wood as the rider let down the gate.

Flattening himself against the wall he could see neither horse nor rider as the pony was led close to the stable shelter. The animal was still out of his angle of vision as he heard the rider drag the saddle off, not three yards away.

Then close beside him the rider appeared, and for a moment was a silhouette against the snow; a figure made shapeless by the shouldered saddle.

Within the stable he could see nothing at all, though the other eased the saddle upon the rack so close at hand that a swinging stirrup struck his knee. So little space separated them that he could hear the rider breathe, could have touched him by raising his hand.

Kentucky Jones said softly, "Put up your hands."

He heard the breath jerk in the other's throat; and for a moment they stood in utter silence, as if neither of them any longer breathed at all. He could not tell whether or not he had been obeyed.

The other said, "Who—who is it?"

The wind went out of Kentucky Jones. The voice was hardly more than a whisper, twisted almost past recognition by shock and strain—but he would have known it anywhere in the world as the voice of Jean Ragland.

For a moment both of them stood motionless in the dark. Then Kentucky Jones said, "What in the name of—" He stepped out from the wall so that he could see her silhouetted figure against the snow outside. Without the saddle there was nothing about her outline to suggest the man he had expected. He had a queer shocked feeling that somehow a substitution had been made by unnatural means, so definitely had he expected Joe St. Marie. Then he saw her sway; and he stepped forward in time to catch her in his arms.

Even then she would have slipped to the ground if he had not held her up. The starch had gone out of her and she stood limp, not inert but trembling violently.

"Don't—don't ever do anything like that again," she gasped at last.

"Good Lord! Do you think I had any idea it was you?"

She freed herself and stood unsteadily on braced legs. "What on earth were you trying to do?"

"I thought—I thought you were Joe St. Marie."

"St. Marie."

"I saw someone slide out of here on the horse St. Marie rode today. I saw that horse come back, and I saw its rider talk to Bob Elliot, on his big paint."

The shock of surprise she had sustained in the dark was turning into anger. "And what did you think you were going to do about it?" she demanded.

72

"That hardly matters now, does it?"

"I asked you a question," she said hotly.

"I'll answer it then. If anybody but you had gone wolf prowling out of here in the night to powwow with your father's worst enemy, and I caught him at it—I'd have had the reason for that out of him, if I had to choke it out of him with these two hands."

Jean's anger wilted. "You're bad luck for me," she whispered. "Everything that you have anything to do with goes wrong for me."

"Maybe," he said, "that's because I don't know what you're trying to do."

"Why should I tell you what I'm trying to do?"

"No reason; except that it seems to work out badly when you don't."

She turned to him sharply. She was standing very close to him in the dark, but her words were so faint that he could hardly make them out. "I can tell you this," she said, "I know what I'm doing here. I know more about what's happening here than you can possibly know. Can't you trust that? Haven't you any faith in me at all?"

"You still won't tell me what you're trying to do?"

"I can't! I can't possibly do that."

## CHAPTER SEVEN

All day long the Bar Hook had tried to reach Sheriff Floyd Hopper without success; he had lost himself somewhere among the ranchers who had no phones. Campo Ragland was unwilling to take up the death of Sanders—with its definite implication that Mason had been murdered—with any of the deputies. And the case hung fire, awaiting Hopper's return to Waterman.

But when word reached the sheriff at last, two hours after dark, he lost no time in getting on the job. That day Campo Ragland had put all hands except Jones and Bishop on the road to Waterman with his five carloads of long twos; and since the beeves had trampled the road open as they went, the sheriff was able to drive steaming into the Bar Hook within an hour of his first notice.

Floyd Hopper came into the kitchen briskly, his flat loose-skinned jowls reddish-purple from the wind; and though he grinned at them ruefully as he tried to rub the frost out of his mustache, his eyes were wary, and did not smile at all.

"So poor Zack has turned up at last," he said, warming his hands over the stove. "How come you to find him, Lee?"

"My horse kept shying one particular place," Lee Bishop said. "Soon as Kentucky called it to my notice I begun to wonder if there wasn't a dead coyote or something under the snow. So Kentucky and me looked, and there he was."

"'Soon as Kentucky called it to your notice,'" the sheriff repeated. "So it was really Kentucky Jones who thought of looking in this place—is that right?"

"Well, yes, though he only said—"

"All right. Could you make out how he died?"

"Fighting," said Bishop. "He was lying in a kind of heap, face down, but partly on his side. He'd been shot twice, once in the left side, and once in the back. His gun was under him in his right hand, and it was fired three times."

"His gun belt—" began the sheriff.

"He didn't wear a gun belt—didn't own one, far's I know—just carried his gun in his pocket, I guess."

The sheriff nodded. "Let's see his gun, then." As Lee Bishop went out, the sheriff turned to Kentucky Jones. "Could you tell which way Zack was firing when he went down?"

Kentucky exhaled smoke and shook his head. "A man's liable to spin and fall most any way, when he's hit."

"Zack was lying beside a rock, wasn't he? Now, the trail from down-canyon comes past that stone pump house. Did it look to you like he might have took cover behind that rock, to fire down the trail?"

"That could hardly be," Kentucky answered.

"Why?"

"Because he lay on the down-trail side."

"Which way—" The sheriff broke off abruptly as Lee Bishop returned to the room with Zack Sanders' six-gun. He took a quick stride forward and took the gun in his hand.

"What's the matter?" Campo Ragland demanded instantly.

The sheriff drew a deep breath and blew it out through puffed cheeks. The eager intensity of inquiry had gone out of him. "I never have any luck," he grunted. "This damn thing has sure worked out to make a fool of everybody!"

"What's wrong with that gun?" said Ragland again.

"Nothing, except the caliber," said the sheriff. "It's a forty-five, that's what's the matter with it. How much snow was there under Zack Sanders?"

"None," said Bishop.

"Lee," said the sheriff, "you found Mason too: could you judge which was killed first? Sanders or Mason?"

"I wouldn't be able to draw any difference."

"Uh huh," said Sheriff Hopper. "This here is the devil."

"It was sure a striking accident," Kentucky agreed. "More like a whole committee of accidents."

"When I first heard of this," the sheriff admitted, "I was hopeful we were out of the woods. Naturally the first thing that came to mind was that Mason and Sanders shot it out, and both dropped. But the caliber of Zack's gun—it throws that theory out."

"Shucks—right back on the double suicide theory," said Kentucky. "But wait a minute!"

"What's the matter?"

"The gun Mason carried was the same caliber as this gun of Sanders' here," Kentucky pointed out. "It passed at the inquest that Mason was killed by the accidental discharge of his own gun. How is it we're so certain now that Mason was not killed by that caliber?"

The sheriff pulled a pipe from his pocket and rammed tobacco into it with a disgusted thumb. "Because," he said, "Mason was not killed by the discharge of his own gun. John Mason was murdered."

They stared at him, and Kentucky Jones heard the breath catch in Jean Ragland's throat.

"How long have you known this?" Campo Ragland demanded at last.

"I've known it," said the sheriff, "since Mason died."

"Then you knew at the inquest—"

Sheriff Floyd Hopper did not avoid the challenging stare of the cattleman. "Yes," he said, "I knew it at the inquest."

There was a fragile and puzzled silence, presently broken by Campo. "Then the coroner's jury wasn't given all the facts?"

"No," said the sheriff.

"I'm damned if I see your idea, Floyd!" said Campo.

Floyd Hopper's temper seemed to flare again. "I had good reasons for steering in a bum verdict at the inquest. But those reasons have gone to hell in a snow storm, now!"

"What I want to know," said Campo Ragland, "is how much more you didn't tell the jury!"

"Not much, Campo. John Mason was killed by two shots—not one—from a gun of lighter caliber than forty-five. Tomorrow the whole country will know that—and our chances of getting the killer are cut in two." He extended his hands over the stove, but promptly withdrew them again, and instead peeled off his coat.

"Naturally," Kentucky put in equably, "it's easier to catch a criminal who thinks he's safe."

"And easier yet," said Campo irritably, "to explain away a killing as an accident!"

"Yes," said the sheriff without heat. He returned Ragland's stare through the smoke cloud from his pipe. "But I also had one or two other reasons. For one thing, this is some worse than just a one-man killing, Campo. It's kicked the whole of Wolf Bench onto the edge of a

77

general smash."

"We all have reason to know that," Ragland growled.

"All right. Suppose now somebody that don't know much about it picks himself out a first class suspect. Suppose, for instance, somebody goes around Wolf Bench pointing out that Lee Bishop just happens to be the man that found both Mason and Sanders—both deep hidden under the snow. There's been many a blow-up on less evidence than that—and with less feeling back of it than this is going to raise up here!"

Lee Bishop said nothing. Campo was eyeing Sheriff Hopper narrowly. "Somehow, Floyd," he said, "it seems like to me you haven't come to your real reason yet."

"No?" said Sheriff Hopper. He took a deep drag on his pipe. "Then I'll give you just one reason more. Maybe you've forgot, Campo, that John Mason was shot down within a dozen horse-jumps of your own house here; and—by singular coincidence—that neither you, nor your daughter, nor a single one of your hands, was even within earshot of the guns."

After a moment Campo said in a low voice, "Floyd, what do you mean by that?"

"Campo, I know that John Mason was your close friend. I know that you and your brand are as bad hurt as anybody is, almost. And with my experience, I can reason that the thing couldn't have happened if any of you *had* been here. But most people hate coincidences, Campo."

Ragland stood up, his face blank. "Floyd, if you're saying you smothered that inquest as a favor to me—"

"Maybe," said the sheriff, "I should just have let you

78

explain all that to the rimrock in your own way."

Campo Ragland sat down, his combativeness abruptly deflated. "Floyd," he said, "you shouldn't have done it."

"Of course to hell I shouldn't have done it!" said the sheriff, his irritability coming to the surface again. "A fine box I'm in, now that Zack Sanders is found!"

"Well, anyway, Floyd," Campo mumbled, "I appreciate what you tried to do."

"All right," the sheriff accepted, "see that you do! Seems to me, Campo, that after this you'd be justified if you'd stop holding information back."

"What do you mean by that?"

"Tonight over the phone I asked you if anything else peculiar had happened. You told me 'No.' But I happen to know that you got home here Tuesday to find that this house had been searched."

Kentucky Jones had never seen Sheriff Floyd Hopper show to as good advantage as he did tonight. Basically the sheriff's mood was disgruntled and ugly; it was not easy for him to face the exposure of his subterfuges. Yet he was the man in the saddle here. He sat now sprawled behind his smoke, his eyes surly and red, like the eyes of a bear. And he had the tough, planted look of gnarled tree roots.

"What house?" said Campo Ragland at last.

"This house," said the sheriff. "What are you trying to do, Campo? It doesn't get you anything to stall with me. This house was searched and something was taken from it."

"If you know that something was taken from this house," Campo Ragland said, "it's because you had it taken yourself."

Hopper shook his head. "All I know is that something is gone from here—and never mind how I know that. I'll have to satisfy you that I do know it."

"It seems," said Campo Ragland, "that you know a lot of things that nobody thought you knew. I'm thinking that maybe you know a lot of things more."

"What you'd better be finding out is this, Campo," said Sheriff Hopper. "I'm no fool, even if I am the duly elected sheriff of Waterman county. You could do a whole lot worse than play a straight game with me."

Campo's retort was mildly explosive. "Straight game? Of course I'm playing a straight game! I'm willing to turn face up what cards I hold—they're always face up. It's not my fault when I hold very damn few cards."

"What I'm saying is—"

The sheriff was interrupted by the opening of the outer door. The strong golden lamplight wavered slightly with the pressure of the cool draft; and to their nostrils came the peculiarly exhilarating smell of the clear cold air from the snow. In the doorway appeared Joe St. Marie. For a moment he hesitated, hand on the latch, obviously startled by the presence of the sheriff.

"Shut that door," said Campo; and Joe St. Marie came in and closed the door slowly behind him.

"What are you doing here?"

Joe St. Marie swung off his hat and stood staring bleakly from Ragland to Hopper and back again. "I lamed my horse," he said. "I had to leave the other boys to take the beef on to Waterman. It would have spoiled the cayuse to go on."

Now Campo Ragland seemed to notice what Kentucky Jones had perceived at once; that Joe St. Marie's face was the color of half-cured hay; and the bronc rider's explanation of his presence, if not altogether satisfactory in itself, had served to draw attention to the quickness of his breath. Campo said sharply, "You hurt, Joe?"

"No sir; no sir, Mr. Ragland."

"What's the matter with you? Are you sick?"

"No sir. I'm all right. Well—I don't feel so good, at that."

"You never feel so good," Lee Bishop grunted.

Campo Ragland hesitated, puzzled. "You want to speak to me, Joe?" he asked at last.

"Who? Me? No, sir."

"Well, see what you can find yourself to eat. Wait a minute—what have you given your horse?"

"Nothing yet, Mr. Ragland, sir. I—"

"How many times do I have to tell you fellers—" Ragland began. "Well, let it pass. Go feed your horse."

"Now?"

"Now!"

Joe St. Marie had already thrown aside his sheepskin coat and hung his gun belt on a wooden peg beside the door. He moved reluctantly at Ragland's command, and at the door he stopped, hesitating. Though he seemed unable to speak, it was as plain as if he had spoken that there was in his mind a protest which he could not—or did not dare—put into words. He swayed indeterminately upon his long horse-bowed legs, making the polished steel studs on his five-inch belt glint in the slant of the light.

81

In spite of the grey-green pallor of St. Marie's face, Kentucky Jones thought he had never seen the Indian blood of the man stand out so strongly. The breadth of face at the cheek-bones and the surface lights in St. Marie's eyes suggested the Indian always; but the blunt strength of his features ordinarily offset this impression. Just now, though, a great part of that strength seemed to be gone.

"Well?" said Campo softly.

St. Marie glanced quickly from Campo to the sheriff, wavering a moment in indecision; then hurriedly took his gun belt from its peg. So, at last, he opened the door and went out, shoulders hunched as if against the great unseen pressure of a non-existent wind.

When St. Marie had left the room there was a moment or two of silence. "It's funny we didn't hear his horse coming up," the sheriff said.

"You often don't," said Ragland, "when you've got loose stock in the corrals."

Without raising his voice the sheriff asked, "What's he afraid of, Campo?"

Campo met his eye grimly. "I was about to ask you."

"You mean you don't know?"

"Floyd, I haven't got the slightest idee. It might be the man is sick."

"That man ain't sick," said Hopper. "The blood was already coming back to his face. Campo, something has happened to that man, just a few minutes before he come into this room."

"Do you suppose—" Campo began.

Somewhere outside the house a gun crashed; and

though they could not judge either its exact direction or distance, they knew that it had been fired within the hundred yards. For a moment they listened. Then Lee Bishop jumped for the door, and they all seemed to move at once.

"Wait, Lee," Campo Ragland snapped. "Blow out those lights, Floyd, Kentuck! Jean, you stay in here, you hear me?"

As the lights went out the small frost-paned windows became faintly visible, blue in the darkness, where a moment before they had been squares of silver-dusted black. Then the door swung open upon the trampled starlit snow and they went out, quick but unhurried, an irregular file of shadows against the pale glimmer of the earth.

Campo Ragland, unarmed, led the way to the corral where Joe St. Marie was most likely to have left his horse. The horse was there, head to the bars, waiting for the feed that had not yet come; but Joe St. Marie was not in sight.

Campo's voice raised in a hoarse shout, an abrupt strange sound in all that silence of snow and rock and stars. "You, Joe! St. Marie! Where you at? Sing out, man!"

The silence held for a moment more, and Campo had whirled upon the sheriff, when Joe St. Marie spoke in an odd muffled voice, unexpectedly nearby. "Yes, sir—here I am."

He came toward them now, slowly, from around the corner of the stable, and Lee Bishop let droop the rifle he had snatched up.

"Who fired?"

"Why—I did." The accent of Joe St. Marie's speech was no different from that of any other cowboy, except for a certain deep thickness of the tone itself. Now his voice was still deep, but it had taken on a flat quality; and though the voice itself did not shake, it somehow conveyed the impression that the man behind it was more than shaken. "I—I thought I seen a wolf."

"Wolf! A wolf up here by the house?"

"Well—I guess it was a coyote then."

"Go on in," Lee Bishop said disgustedly. "I'll see your horse gets fed." This offer St. Marie did not accept; but Lee Bishop stayed behind while the others went in.

"I thought I told you to stay in here," Campo said to his daughter, lighting a lamp.

The sheriff's temper seemed to have come to the end of its string, and there busted itself like a roped steer. "I'm sick and tired of this," he told them. "There's something almightly funny going on here, and I mean to know what it is!"

Campo Ragland planted himself on wide-spread legs, back to the stove. "When you find out," he said sourly, "let me know."

"I've warned you about holding out on me," the sheriff said to Ragland. "But now I warn you again. I mean to get the man that killed Mason. I mean to get him, you hear me?"

Campo Ragland said with sudden passion, "God knows I'll help you every way I can. I tell you, if I knew anything—"

"If you knew anything!" said Hopper bitterly. "There

isn't a man on your place tonight who doesn't know more about this business than he means to tell!"

"That's all foolishness," said Campo Ragland. "You've gone up in the air because a quarter-blood cowboy looks like he might be coming down with a fever. As for holding stuff back from you—take us one by one if you want. Start with me. Or start with Kentucky Jones, who didn't even work for the Bar Hook at the time this happened. Or take—"

"You want me to start with Kentucky Jones?" said the sheriff. "Maybe you'd like to hear me ask a question or two of this Kentucky Jones?"

"Ask who and what you like," said Ragland.

Hopper swung his red-eyed stare to Kentucky. "Be careful how you answer me, Jones; try to remember what your boss sometimes forgets—that maybe I know the answer before you speak. Where were you at one o'clock last Saturday—the day that Mason and Zack Sanders died?"

Kentucky Jones took his time about answering. He took the makings from his pocket and started a cigarette. "One, last Saturday," he repeated "that was just about an hour before the snow began to fall, wasn't it?"

"Some less than an hour, I'd say," the sheriff said.

They waited while Kentucky Jones twirled shut his cigarette, and stuck it in the corner of his mouth. "At noon last Saturday," he said at last, "I was here at the Bar Hook."

Sheriff Hopper grinned, but not pleasantly, at Campo Ragland. "There you are," he said.

There was quiet again; and this time the eyes of

everyone were upon Kentucky Jones. He was meeting Floyd Hopper's stare, and he did not glance at the others; but he could feel them watching him—the beset and irritably wary Campo Ragland, and the girl, whose cross-purpose here he could not yet read.

Campo said slowly, "You never told me that, Kentuck."

"No? I drove out to say *Adios;* I was going away."

Hopper spoke to Ragland. "There's your man that couldn't possibly know anything about this," he said ironically. "But if you think that's all I know about Kentucky Jones, you're a fool. I can go to court with my case against him tomorrow, if need be." His tone was that of contemptuous statement rather than threat. "And I can put him where he'll have to fight hell for leather, as he never fought in his life, before he ever gets clear."

Ragland said, "If you think being here around that time is a case, you don't know much about—"

"Opportunity," said the sheriff. "Opportunity—and motive. Just those two things can make it tough for any man. Yet I'm not right sure that that's all I can bring against him, from what I know right now."

"Motive?" echoed Ragland, startled.

Here Lee Bishop and Joe St. Marie returned to the room.

## CHAPTER EIGHT

They saw now that the normal dark color of St. Marie's face had returned, and with it had come back his look of solid strength. Sheriff Floyd Hopper looked at Ragland and indicated St. Marie with a jerk of his head. "Chills and fever seem to have passed off," he said.

Campo Ragland grunted.

"Campo," said the sheriff, "there's a head going to fall—maybe more than one head. Don't ever think that this is going to blow over, and be lost sight of in a general dust. There's a man going to be hooked hard and permanent before I'm through."

"Floyd, what are you going to do? You mean you're taking Kentucky Jones?"

"No. I'll know how to get him when I want him, I think. Now make your choice, Campo! If you don't want to string with me, I can go on without you. But you may not like your choice before this thing is through."

"I don't know what you mean," said Ragland.

"Suit yourself," said Hopper; "only, don't be too sure that this case is shaping up against Kentucky Jones."

Ragland angered again. "Look here, Floyd—I'm plenty tired of this. You can't come in here and talk that way to me! I'm not going to stand for it, you hear me?"

"Have it your own way, Campo." The sheriff picked up his coat and gloves.

"You're not going back to Waterman tonight, are you?" Jean exclaimed.

"Sure I'm going back. There's nothing I can do out here."

Nobody urged him to stay. Campo Ragland asked what Hopper wanted them to do about Zack Sanders, and received instructions for reporting in Waterman for an inquest. No great warmth of understanding marked Hopper's departure.

"If you change your mind, Campo," the sheriff said,

"let me know."

"I tell you I don't know what you're talking about!" Campo said stubbornly; and the sheriff took the long trail back to town.

Stamping back into the house, Campo Ragland turned immediately upon Joe St. Marie. The swarthy bronc rider was filling himself up on bread and cold meat; and he met Campo's questions with a stolid gaze.

"What's got into you, St. Marie?"

"I don't feel so good."

"Look here, St. Marie—if something funny has happened around here I want to know what it is."

"I don't feel so good."

"Who did you throw down on when you went out to feed your horse?"

"Who? Me?"

Campo Ragland exploded at him. "Yes, you! Who did you fire at? Come out with it, now!"

"I thought I saw a coyote," said St. Marie.

"Don't lie to me! You can't get away with that stuff here!"

"I don't feel so good."

Campo Ragland gave it up in disgust, and St. Marie hurriedly took himself out of range, retiring to the bunk house.

Campo seemed bewildered. To Kentucky Jones it seemed that the cross purposes which held the boss of the Bar Hook in a state of paralysis were now almost physically visible, as wind is visible in prairie hay by its effect. Here was an owner whose range was being swamped, overwhelmed by the herds of his enemy; he faced a ruin which could only be averted by an immediate and determined contest for the ground. Yet something had thrown and hog-tied this man—some obscure and hidden circumstance which he seemed at a loss to combat. Kentucky no longer could doubt that the circumstance which hog-tied Ragland had to do with Jean.

"I'll hire a cook when we go in for the inquest." Ragland spoke tonelessly, like a man seeking escape from other things. "Jean wants to do the cooking, and I'll let her, I guess; but you fellers will have to get the fires started in the morning. I'm not going to have her slamming firewood around at any 4:00 A.M."

"I'll take first crack at it," said Lee Bishop.

Kentucky Jones saw his chance and jumped it. The ultimate answer might be deep in twisted trails, but his next step was obvious and immediate—he had to force the truth out of St. Marie. Lee Bishop's removal would make opportunity for this, since the other hands would not be back from Waterman until the cars had been loaded in the morning. "Then take the bunk off the kitchen, Lee," he said. "I'll run down and get you your bed."

Down in the bunk house, to which Joe St. Marie had retired, no light showed; but from within came the complicated rhythms of a mouth organ played by a master, telling Kentucky that his man was still there, and awake. Joe St. Marie could make a mouth organ sob and whimper, or imitate a herd of steers or a railway train. The mouth organ fell silent, however, as he approached; and, Kentucky stepping into the full light of no less than three lamps, saw that blankets screened the windows;

89

and a six-gun had replaced the mouth organ in Joe St. Marie's hands.

"Oh, it's you," said St. Marie sheepishly, and dropped the six-gun on the bunk beside him.

"I was hoping you got that guy, Joe," said Kentucky. "Didn't you even wing him?"

The queer mouthing complaint of the harmonica stopped for a moment as St. Marie looked sharply at Kentucky over his cupped hands. He did not, however, take the mouth organ from his mouth.

Kentucky cast a glance at the blankets which screened the windows. "Look here. If I'm going to sleep in this bunk house I want to know who you thought was going to fire through the window."

"I hung those up to keep the cold wind out," said St. Marie.

"You don't figure to tell me, huh?"

"Nothing to tell."

"You look here, Joe! If ever a man was scared, you were when you came into that kitchen tonight. Now I want to know what lifted you out of your boots."

St. Marie considered briefly, then shrugged. "It wasn't anything; you'd laugh."

"Try it out, anyway."

Joe St. Marie grunted, planted his elbows on his bowed knees and humped over his harmonica again. The instrument let out a low quavering blat.

"And what was it drew your fire, out there by the corral?"

St. Marie did not answer; he had retreated into the stolidity possible to his darker forbears.

Kentucky, stepping to the edge of the bunk, smoothly lifted the six-gun from St. Marie's side and tossed it into another bunk. The music stopped short.

Kentucky said, "Now—you—talk!"

Joe St. Marie slid his high heels under him, bunched himself as if he were going to start his music again; then the harmonica dropped to the floor as he uncoiled and sprang.

Kentucky dropped into a crouch and laced out with a long uppercutting wallop. Two seconds later St. Marie was on his back between the stove and the wall, while Kentucky held him down with a knee on the bronc rider's chest. "Now you be good," he said. "By God, you fool with me, I'll snap you like a whip!"

St. Marie made a desperate effort to rise. "In God's name, Jones, there's somebody coming!"

"I don't care if there's a regiment coming. You're going to sit quiet and pretty until we talk this over."

"Then take my gun! Take my gun yourself," Joe St. Marie urged him. "You want to die?"

The honest fear in Joe St. Marie was not for Kentucky, he now recognized; undoubtedly it was for the approach beyond the door. "All right," said Kentucky disgustedly. He left the bronc rider, recovered St. Marie's gun, and stuck it negligently in his waistband. There was a low tapping at the door.

"Come in!"

The door opened quickly, but not wide, and Jean Ragland slid in. She shut the door and leaned against it, her hands behind her upon the latch. She wore no coat. "What's the matter here?" she demanded.

"Joe and I were wrestling," said Kentucky. "What's broke loose, Miss Ragland?"

"Nothing's broke loose." Her blue eyes looked almost black, but the yellow lamp light turned her hair into a glowing smoulder, as if there were fire in it. "All right, Joe—I can't stay here forever; what happened tonight?"

Jean Ragland spoke without sharpness; but her question was an order which she obviously did not suspect would be disobeyed. Joe St. Marie dropped his eyes and swayed from side to side like a steer baffled by a fence. "Aw, Miss Ragland—"

"Come out with it now!"

Joe St. Marie squirmed. "You wouldn't believe—"

"Never mind that."

The bronc rider could not escape Jean Ragland's waiting eyes. Suddenly he blurted out his answer.

"I seen a ghost! Miss Ragland, I swear to heaven, I seen the ghost of John Mason, as plain as I see you stand there now!"

The girl was silent a moment, astounded by St. Marie's idiotic answer. "For heaven's sake, Joe, pull yourself together! If some rider has been into this layout I want to know—"

"Miss Ragland," St. Marie insisted, "I've got good eyes. I don't forget. I know most of the cattle on this range by sight at a half mile. You think I don't remember how Old Ironsides used to set, half crooked in the saddle with his shoulders hunched—you think I wouldn't know him out of a thousand men—"

It was Jean Ragland that Kentucky Jones was watching; and now he saw that comprehension had come to her. She seemed to stiffen, and her eyes looked even darker than before.

"I saw it twice," Joe St. Marie was rushing on now. "The first time sitting out there on the hump; and again when I went out to feed my horse, farther out, going down the trail. I fired at it—and it disappeared."

"All right, Joe. Was that all you saw?"

"Good God, Miss Ragland, wasn't that enough?"

Jean Ragland drew a deep unsteady breath. "Yes—I expect it was. You'd better keep this to yourself, Joe, if you know what's good for you." She added, "Both of you." She sent Kentucky Jones a glance that might have been an appeal; then suddenly turned and let herself out the door. Kentucky Jones hesitated, and opened his mouth to ask Joe St. Marie a question; then, changing his mind, he followed her.

At the sound of the door Jean turned and waited; he fell in beside her and walked with her to the house.

"Miss Ragland," he said, "who, besides yourself, knows what Joe St. Marie saw tonight?"

She turned on him quickly. "Do you?"

"No; it was just a question."

"Listen," she said. "Listen. I've got to tell you this: When I—when I gave you that bullet—I swear I didn't know you had been here the day—the day Mason was killed. If I'd thought there was the least chance of your getting bogged down in this thing—"

"Am I bogged down?"

"Can't you see what Floyd Hopper means to do? Right or wrong—he'll see somebody roped. And that means more than just the sheriff against—the man he picks. All

Wolf Bench will rise up to back the sheriff's play, without justice, without mercy—"

"We won't worry about that, just yet."

"But I tell you, Kentucky, if I'd only known— Is it true that he can show you had a reason to kill Mason?"

He considered. "Yes," he said.

"What can I say?" Her whisper came to him brokenly. "What can I say?"

"How did you first know that Mason was murdered?" he asked.

She said in a smothered voice, "I can't tell you now."

"Did you know that Zack Sanders was dead?"

"No! I didn't know! I never guessed—"

"Then—"

"Don't! Don't ask me any more. I can't—I can't—"

"Child," he said gently, "you don't need to tell me anything you don't feel like telling me, now or any other time."

She said in a half-choked voice, "It's my fault that you're here."

"If there's anything I can do to make things go any easier for you, I want to do it. And I don't blame you for wishing I was out of this. But—"

"No," she said, "no, I want you to stay here."

He said to himself, "Good Lord, she means to use me yet!" Aloud he said, "Then that's all right."

She spoke with difficulty. "This—this is the meanest thing I ever did in my life."

"What is?"

She did not answer him; but instead she unexpectedly crooked an elbow around his neck, pulled down his

94

head, and kissed his mouth.

When she was gone he stood for a moment or two in the snow, considering. Far off somewhere a timber wolf howled, the first he had heard in half a dozen years.

# CHAPTER NINE

Had it stood alone, the shooting of Zack Sanders, a crippled ranch cook, might have passed with little notice, and the inquest it occasioned might have been a routine and almost perfunctory performance. But the obvious— and at the same time extremely elusive—connection between the killing of Sanders and the death of John Mason stirred new war talk throughout the length of the rimrock.

Caught between a falling beef market and the heavy death losses of three years' drought, the rimrock cattlemen were in no shape to face the injury to their credit system resulting from the death of Mason. Even while it was generally supposed that Mason had died by the accidental discharge of his own gun, the temper of the rimrock cattlemen had been stormy and insecure. Now suddenly they were asked to accept the news that Mason's death had been no accident; that the redoubtable Old Ironsides had been murdered by parties unknown.

Twenty-four hours after Lee Bishop discovered the body of Zack Sanders under the snow, the whole rimrock knew both the discovery and its meaning. Fully as many people swarmed into Waterman for the inquest upon the shooting of Zack Sanders as had gathered for the Mason inquest. But this time the people showed a different mood. The death of Mason had left the cattle people irritable, but dazed and uncertain. The proof of murder turned them ugly. Sheriff Hopper had expected this revelation to arouse a certain amount of criticism and dispute; but he had under-estimated the difficulty of his position at least seventy-five per cent.

And while the cattlemen were making it hot for Sheriff Hopper in Waterman, there had sprung up among the cattlemen themselves an even more uncertain situation. The circumstances of Mason's murder had already made the Bar Hook the focal point of the general disaster. The incredibly prompt and bold decisions of Bob Elliot's threatened 88 now promised to make the Bar Hook the focal point of the sequel. Whatever could be said against Bob Elliot, he was proving now that he could make a decision that popped like a blacksnake whip. The 88's first drive of cattle was already spread all over the middle of the Bar Hook range, cutting heavily into the feed that the Bar Hook Herefords would need long before the spring.

Yet, now, of all times in his career, Campo Ragland chose this to go into what appeared to be a black and hopeless funk.

The boss of the Bar Hook was habitually red-eyed now, and the curve of his forehead was no longer a bland majestic sweep. He looked as if he might at any moment spit red hot pebbles. Four times in two days Lee Bishop had urged his boss to turn his riders loose upon the encroaching herds of the 88 and as a reward for this had been the victim of as many surly explosions. Campo's unaccountable vacillation was breaking the morale of them all.

The day after the inquest Kentucky Jones got back from the morning's work before the rest. He found Jean in the kitchen, up to her elbows in flour and dough. The cook that Campo Ragland had hired in Waterman had failed to show; and Campo Ragland, more and more inclined to let things drift from day to day, had not yet succeeded in the monumental task of getting another one out.

Jean's eyes quickened instantly as Kentucky Jones came in. "Are the others back?"

"Not yet."

"Come here," she commanded. "I have to talk to you."

"Just a second." He went to the phone and belled the gunsmith at Waterman.

Old Mark Ferris, Wolf Bench gunsmith for more than twenty years, knew most of the guns in the Waterman rimrock; and Kentucky had talked to him the day before in an effort to trace the ownership of the gun found in Zack Sanders' hand. It had seemed to him odd that Zack, who owned no gun belt, should have been carrying a gun; and he had been led to wonder if Zack could have been forewarned, and had perhaps borrowed the weapon. If this were true, he wanted to know whose gun Zack had borrowed. Therefore he had set Ferris searching through his records for the serial number of the questioned gun, in the hope that the old gunsmith could recall to whom the gun had been sold.

Presently Mark Ferris' voice came over the wire, querulous and faint. "I can't find any record of that gun," he said. "I don't believe I ever sold that gun, Kentuck."

"You must have sold it," Kentuck insisted. "Look here,

Ferris—this is no joke! Look again!"

"All right."

Kentucky hung up and went to sit opposite Jean at the table where she was at work, and began the making of a cigarette.

"I suppose by this time," she began, "you have no end of theories about what happened here."

"No," he said.

"That's funny; everyone else has."

"I used to know an old lion hunter, name of Old Man Coffee," Kentucky told her. "Whenever a killing or something had everybody else balled up, they used to send for Old Man Coffee. He didn't always unravel the trail; but he seemed to see through a lot of things that fooled other folks. And once I asked him how he did it."

"And he told you?"

"He said he made things easy for himself by never having a theory—he just kept hunting up facts, and when he had enough to give him the answer, there wasn't any theory about it—he knew."

"And that was *his* theory," said Jean.

"Maybe. But me, I think Old Man Coffee's way was a good way."

She stopped work and studied him. "I can't make you out," she said at last. "You mean—you have no idea of your own who killed Mason—or Zack Sanders—or why?"

"Miss Ragland—Jean," he said slowly, "I think you don't want me to know those answers."

She said quickly, "Why do you say that?"

"Child," he said, "how long is it going to be before you

tell somebody—anybody—what you know?"

She looked at him suddenly as she answered, and he knew that she lied to him, bravely, and with open eyes. "I haven't the least idea what you mean," she said.

"All right. But I ought to tell you this—if I stay here much longer, I'll know who killed Mason—and why."

"You—you're sure of that?"

"The facts I have are very few," he said. "I don't know where they lead. But already I know they lead a clear straight trail."

"How can you—why do you know that?"

"The facts are too distinct and clear to be pointing more than one way. Those two men killed at the same time, but by two different calibers of guns; this house being searched; the fact that the two were killed at almost the same time, but were found lying nearly sixty yards apart—each thing stands out sharp as the slot of a deer in the snow. When those facts are finally fitted together nobody will ever be able to blur them so that there's any doubt."

"If you're going to turn yourself into a spy—" Jean began hotly. She stopped, checked by the steadiness of his regard.

Kentucky Jones said gently, "Who are you shielding, Jean?"

She straightened and stood looking out through the clear space in the middle of the frosted pane. She was bleak-eyed, and her face was passive, but her head was up with a fine proud carriage, and her hair was smoky flame. "I'm glad it's over with," she said at last. "Sooner or later you were bound to ask that, of course."

"Of course," he repeated. He could not see that there was any sign of faltering in this girl. It was as if she could expect her whole world to come down around her in a rattling avalanche if ever she lost her grip.

"You hardly expected any answer, I suppose?"

"No," he admitted.

She turned her eyes to look at him slowly, curiously. "I suppose the answer to that is another thing that you are sure to know, if you stay."

"Of course," he said again.

She drew a deep unsteady breath. "I—I was trying to talk to you about something else."

"I'm sorry, Jean."

She looked at him hard. "It's nearly noon," she said. "In a few minutes the riders will be coming in. Tell me this, Kentucky: if you were boss of the Bar Hook, could you save the brand?"

"I only know one way. It's a way that most men would hesitate to take."

"And what is that?"

"To feed Elliot his own medicine. It would mean more riders; all of them tough, trouble-hunting men. It would be their job to run those 88 brand cattle back where they came from; and run them again next week, and the week after, and every time they come—run them till their bones rattle. But if a man thinks he might be squeamish about seeing empty saddles come in—then he might better hesitate some, before he takes that way."

"Would you?" she asked him. "Would you hesitate?"

"If it was my brand—no."

"Listen." She leaned toward him, her hands on the

table. "My father isn't going to fight."

"Not now, you mean?"

"Not now, nor later, nor ever."

"Jean," said Kentucky, "is it you that's keeping him from making his fight?"

She hesitated, as if she truly did not know how to answer. "Yes," she said uncertainly at last. Then after a moment she changed it. "No," she said. "I kept Campo out of a fight once; maybe it was a fight that he should have made. But it's out of my hands now, Kentuck."

"You sure don't give me much to go on," Kentucky said. "But I'll say this: if ever he's going to make his fight, now is the time; every day that he puts it off makes it harder in every way. If he puts it off long enough Elliot will have every chance to win."

A look of forlorn desperation came into her face. "If the Bar Hook was in your hands—do you think you could make a fight that would stand Elliot off?"

"Are you trying to sell me the Bar Hook?"

"What good would that do? There isn't a cattleman in the world who would be fool enough to buy the outfit now. But even if we could sell it, that would be almost as bad as to lose it altogether. Campo is rooted too deep in Wolf Bench cattle. If he loses the Bar Hook he'll never amount to anything again. You can't understand that, for you've never taken root. But Campo—I'd almost as soon see him dead."

"Then—?"

"Listen," she said intensely. She dropped her elbows to the table, bringing her face nearer his, and her words came tumbling out in an intense whisper. "I own a fifth share of the Bar Hook, in my own name. There's no question of selling the brand. But I could sell you my fifth share. Take it in the form of so many hundred grade steers—you to make the cut; or in any form you want. Would you take it?"

He stalled for time, puzzled. "How much are you asking?" he said.

"One dollar," Jean answered.

He stared at her. "And a string to it?"

"This: delivery will not be until next spring; and the cut will be based upon the valuation of the cattle on the range at that time."

He rolled a cigarette, considering. "See if I get this straight," he said. "You're offering me your share of the Bar Hook to make the fight that your father won't make—or can't make. Is that it?"

"Yes," she said. She was very pale. "Lee Bishop can't do anything—he's just a hired foreman and can only carry out Campo's orders. But if you own part of the cattle, with winter grazing rights on the Bar Hook range—then you're justified in protecting your own interests, even though Campo doesn't defend his. I don't think Bob Elliot will fight; I think he'll let his cattle drift back to their home range. But first he has to know he's up against a man that will fight him clear into the ground."

Kentucky sat studying the slow blue tendrils of smoke from his cigarette.

"The deal won't be questioned," Jean said. "You're known to have enough money to buy into a brand if you want to. And nobody can look at you without knowing that whatever you set your hand to you'll fight through some way—maybe just for the love of fighting, for all I know."

Kentucky Jones grinned, but the grin was very faint. He was pitying this girl as he had never pitied anyone in his life. There was a forlorn desperation about her scheme which told him, better than anything else could have done, how heavily events had pressed down upon this girl. In effect, Jean Ragland was offering him all the tangible assets which she controlled to serve as a gunfighter, and a leader of gunfighters. Yet to the best of his belief she was justified. There was nothing imaginary about the encroachment of Elliot; and if Campo persisted in his unaccountable state of paralysis the Bar Hook brand was done.

"What's Campo going to say to this?" he asked her.

"I'll take care of Campo."

He looked up at her. Her eyes were sober and quiet, the blue of distant foothills at dusk. He thought that she was trying to keep from them any suggestion of personal appeal—but that she did not quite succeed.

Kentucky Jones found himself deeply stirred. Yet he would have thought himself a fool if he had accepted such a proposition only to please Jean. One consideration alone urged him to agree. He was anxious to talk to Bob Elliot; and he felt that the basis she suggested would give him every advantage in this.

"I'm not going to turn you down," he said at last. "But I can accept only on certain conditions. First, that too strenuous an objection is not made by your father."

"I hope to be able to handle that."

"Another condition is that if Campo Ragland later decides to make his own fight, or if for any other reason I'm no longer needed, then I can withdraw, and the deal is off."

"I accept that," she said.

"Another condition is that the price of one dollar be changed to read: 'One dollar and such other consideration as the buyer shall consider proper, according to the state of the market upon delivery.'"

She objected vigorously to that; but since at worst it conceded him what profit he might consider justified, she at length gave in.

"One thing more," he said. "If I'm going to make this fight, then I want you to join your mother in California."

She looked at him squarely. "That I will not do."

She stood fast, and he was compelled to give in. When she had won this point she offered him her hand, closing a bargain which placed him in the most curious position he ever had occupied in his life.

"Jean," he said. "If this thing goes through, I'm headed into the middle of something I don't understand—can't understand from what I know. I'm going to ask you one question, and I want you to answer it. Do you know who killed John Mason?"

"No," she said instantly. "Kentucky, I swear that I don't know that! I thought I knew, until Zack Sanders was found; but now I'm just as sure that I was wrong."

"I won't try to get you to tell me," he said, "what you evidently don't want me to know. But, Jean, I tell you this: the time may come when I'll need your help and need it bad. When that time comes, I want you to remember that perhaps I wouldn't be in this if you hadn't asked me in."

"I won't forget."

He got up and jerked on his coat. "I'm going to see Bob Elliot," he told her.

Her hand flew to her mouth. "Now?" she said faintly.

"It's as good a time as any, isn't it?"

Jean Ragland turned white. "Then go on. You—I guess you know I wish you luck."

"I might need it," he admitted.

As he reached the door she suddenly called his name, and he turned back. She was staring after him, white-faced. "Are—will you be armed?"

"I don't know. We'll see."

He was wondering, as he saddled a fresh pony, if she had commissioned him to kill Bob Elliot.

## CHAPTER TEN

The buildings of the 88 were made variously of adobe, clapboards, and square-hewn logs. The layout could not be called compact; yet somehow it had a stripped look, barrenly efficient.

Bill McCord stood in the doorway of the barn as Kentucky Jones came up. Kentucky had a feeling that he had been seen and watched from a long way off.

"You want to see me?" McCord asked.

"I'll talk to your boss, if he's here."

Bill McCord rolled a crooked cigarette from one corner of his mouth to the other. "All right. He's up at the house." He did not offer any accommodations for Kentucky's horse.

Kentucky rode to what appeared to be the main door of a squat adobe which a glance of McCord's eye had indicated. The door opened as he pulled up, and Bob Elliot stood there, looking at him without expression.

"Helly, Bob," Kentucky said.

Bob Elliot leaned against the side of the doorway, lean-shouldered, straight-backed, looking competent and tall. "It seems very peculiar," he said with casual frostiness, "to see you here."

"I suppose so," said Kentucky, swinging down without invitation. "Are you going to ask me in or not?"

"I hadn't thought of it," said Elliot; "is there any special call for it?"

"There is."

"Let's hear what your business is, then."

"It's a little matter of range rights," Kentucky told him.

"In that case," said Elliot, "go back and tell your boss you fell down. I understand my rights on the Bake Pan, and Wolf Bench too, just as well as he does. And when he wants to talk to me he can come himself!"

"Ragland," said Kentucky, "can speak on his own behalf, what and where he wants to, without advice from me—or from you either. It happens that this time I'm speaking for myself. I came over to tell you that I've bought a fifth interest in the Bar Hook."

Bob Elliot's face went blank with perfectly real astonishment. "You bought a—what?"

"You heard me, I think."

Bob Elliot stared at him for a moment more. "Come in here," he said at last. He turned his back and walked into the house; and Kentucky followed him. "I thought I understood you to say you'd bought into the Bar Hook," said Elliot as soon as the door was shut. "Now what in all hell can be your idea in that?"

"I was able to buy some hundreds of head of Bar Hook cattle at a very favorable price," Kentucky told him. "I'll make something on those cattle in the spring."

"In the spring," Elliot repeated. "And where did you expect to hold them through the winter?"

"Right where they are."

Bob Elliot stared at him again while this soaked in. Then abruptly, unexpectedly, he turned away from Kentucky Jones and began to laugh, as Kentucky had seen him laugh before in Sheriff Hopper's office at Waterman. There is no laughter so mirthfully sincere as that which defies its owner's effort to suppress it; and though Bob Elliot's face showed something more like pain than mirth, his laughter had that sincerity now. He pressed the back of his hand to his mouth and seemed to fight the paroxysm, which shook him as if he had been trying to strangle a fit of coughing. "This is rich," he said at last. "Nothing trivial about this transaction, I hope?"

"Hardly."

"So now naturally you want to talk to me."

"Naturally. Both technically and practically, for the time being I am a part owner of the Bar Hook. More particularly as regards the Bar Hook grazing rights."

"Of course you recognize," said Bob Elliot, "that you and I probably don't see eye to eye on grazing rights."

"We can understand each other without going into that very much, I think," Kentucky said. "When it comes to this herd you've shoved onto Bar Hook range—"

"Look here, Jones," Elliot said. "Your object is to bring these cattle you've bought through the winter in good condition, I suppose."

"I mean to bring 'em through."

"Well, you've got one chance to get out of this," said Elliot. "Cut your cattle out of the Bar Hook herds. Lease you a good piece of ground, and take your cattle there. I'll tell you frankly, Jones; it's going to be a tough winter for the Bar Hook herds where they are now."

"I'll leave them where they are," said Kentucky again. "I've already told you I'm swinging with the Bar Hook."

"In short," said Elliot, "what you came here to tell me is that your share in the Bar Hook is a fighting share."

"You can call it that."

Bob Elliot lighted a tailor-made cigarette. His keen knife-carved face was not exactly smiling; but behind it Kentucky Jones now perceived that there was a smouldering satisfaction, a grim content. The ironically humorous glance of his frosty blue eyes had a snap like the flick of a whip. "That girl certainly got you in for something," he said.

"Yes?" Kentucky Jones smiled on one side of his mouth. Until now neither had mentioned the incident in the sheriff's office which had terminated when Kentucky Jones had knocked Bob Elliot out. He held his peace, and began the making of a cigarette; but he thought that Elliot must have known what was in his mind.

"I'll tell you a couple of things for your own good," Bob Elliot went on, half sitting on the edge of a table; his penetrating blue eyes watched Kentucky through the smoke of his cigarette. "You're butting into a situation that you know very little about, Jones. You seem to think that this little difference of opinion that's coming up now between me and Ragland is something new. It isn't. We've had it all the time. Even without this new crisis brought on by Mason's death, there never could have been room for both the Bar Hook and the 88, in the long run. Sooner or later one or the other would have had to go. Up until now I've been willing to give Ragland a break for the sake of the peace. It just happens that the way things fall out I'm not able to baby him any more. Don't you forget for a minute that the land in question is public domain."

"And that you're entitled to graze half way from your water to his. You'll have to govern your cattle count by that; and we don't want to see one head more."

Elliot made an impatient gesture with his cigarette. "It'll be a long day," he said contemptuously, "when you tell me something about the cattle business in the rimrock, Jones. If you think Ragland has a case—ask Campo why he's sitting back in his corner, and sending you to make his bluff. Ask him. You might find out something you need to know."

Kentucky Jones shrugged. "I can't speak for what Campo will do. I've bought in on the understanding that the land my cattle are on is Bar Hook range—has always been Bar Hook range. I'll tell you straight out, Elliot—I don't mean to have that range forced. And if I have to take my boys and ram your stock right back down your throat, in order to hold my graze, stand from under! It's up to you."

Bob Elliot eyed him speculatively. "I haven't the least doubt," he decided, "that you'd run hog wild and make a lot of trouble for yourself and everybody else—once given the chance. No horse on earth is so dangerous to ride as a blind horse. I don't think, though, that you're going to make much of a war on the 88."

"I'll make what push I need to, no more—and no less."

Elliot allowed himself a faint smile. "I suppose you know you'll have to fight Campo himself, first?"

"What makes you think so?"

"For one thing," Elliot told him, "because when you hooked up with Campo Ragland you hooked up with a yellow quitter."

"I reckon," said Kentucky, "you might not be so quick to say that to Campo's face."

"You think not? I'll tell you one more thing you don't know about. I understand that you heard Bill McCord cuss out Lee Bishop, and send him home with his tail between his legs. Well, you can take it that Bill was only copying after his boss. Because this range has seen the day when I sent Campo Ragland home with his tail between his legs, under much the same circumstances. And that wasn't so long ago. Not so long ago!"

"It kind of stumps a man to swallow that one, Elliot— seeing that you're still alive."

"Oh, it does, does it?" Elliot smiled in an ugly way. "Campo went home to get his gun, aiming to kill me. If you want to see Campo bust a cinch, ask him why he never carried that through!"

"This gets no place," said Kentucky. "I told you what

I came to tell you—that lets me out. From now on look to yourself. And don't drive cattle into Bar Hook range—my range—without expecting them to come right home to roost in a cloud of yells."

"Suits me," Elliot agreed. "Don't think I've forgotten the sore jaw you gave me in that run-in at Waterman. God knows I never hoped for such a chance to smash the two of you at once!"

Kentucky Jones grinned and turned to the door. "That's what I like to hear!" He stepped out to his horse.

"Go tell that girl," said Elliot from the door, "that her father can't hide behind you this trip—you ain't big enough in size. And—try and make her tell you what she knows!"

Kentucky was ready to admit—to himself—that that parting shot went home. What he could not escape from was the sure knowledge that Jean Ragland did know something, perhaps several things, which he should have known. He was working precariously and in the dark. But he returned Bob Elliot's sardonic grin.

"Come and see me some time," he said; and he went away from there. . . .

That was a good long-stepping horse Kentucky rode that day; so that it was still a little before the long winter dusk as he reached the half way point on his return ride. He was on the part of the trail which followed the rim, and two miles short of the point where it turned across Wolf Bench to the Bar Hook layout, when his pony pricked its ears forward sharply, and Kentucky brought the horse to a stop while he listened.

Far ahead—whether it came from the Bake Pan or the

Bench he could not tell—sounded a curious drum tattoo, a thin popping whisper of gunfire. The tricky echoes of the rim caught that sound, shook it, and tossed it into the wind curiously broken and prolonged; it seemed to rise and fall, so that a man could not count the number of guns, nor how often they were fired, but could only say that the firing was rapid and from several guns.

For perhaps half a minute the far-off gun talk continued, oddly like the popping of grease in a skillet. Then it stopped abruptly, as if all of the guns had fallen silent together, and in the utter quiet of those vast snowy spaces there was no longer any indication that anything had happened. Kentucky Jones felt a short ugly stir in the pit of his stomach, such as a man feels sometimes when he knows that someone is hurt, perhaps killed, in an event of unknown character.

All that he could be definitely sure of was that the sound of the guns had come from somewhere ahead. He struck the spurs to his horse and went up the irregular trail at the dead run, unbuttoning his coat as he rode so that it would not interfere with his gun.

He rode a mile, a mile and a half; his hard-run horse was snorting visible puffs of frosty breath, like smoke, at every jump. From somewhere ahead of him in the trail came a muffled ground murmur, inarticulate and confused. He pulled his horse down to a gait at which he could listen to something beside his own pony's hoofs. The sound ahead developed swiftly into the hoof-drum of an approaching horse, that supremely stirring, unmistakable sound of a horse running desperately, full stretch, half frantic under the punishment of spur and quirt.

Kentucky Jones hesitated, then put his horse ahead again at a high lope. Within two furlongs the approaching horse burst suddenly from around a jutting outcrop of rock; and he saw that the rider was Jean Ragland.

So close were they as they became visible to each other that as they pulled up their horses Jean's pony slipped to its haunches and almost went down. It recovered itself, however, and the two horses stood blowing and stirring restively on their feet, too steamy and nervous from their running to stand quiet.

"Jean! What's busted?"

She spoke rapidly but with clear coherence. "Jim Humphreys and Billy Petersen have run foul of four 88 cowboys, down on the Bake Pan. Lee Bishop and I were sitting on the rim—we saw the whole thing. Jim Humphreys is down. And they got Billy's horse—he took cover behind his dead horse and began firing back. Oh, God, Kentucky—it was terrible! Sitting there and seeing it all, and unable to do anything—as if we were in another world—"

"Is Billy hit?"

"I don't know. Billy's horse bolted and went into a bucking fit; they were all peppering at him, but he got control of his horse and rode back to cover Jim. Then his horse somersaulted, and the 88 cowboys drew off as he fired from cover."

"Where's Lee Bishop?"

"He's riding down the rim trail to Billy and Jim, fit to break his neck. He wanted me to ride like the devil and get help. I didn't think the others would be back home yet, so I came down this trail hoping to pick you up."

"Come on," said Kentucky, jumping his horse up the trail. Jean put her horse into the trail behind him and they pushed on a steady run to where the fork of the trail led on the one hand precipitously down the rim and on the other up the Bench to the Bar Hook. Here Kentucky stopped his horse and Jean pulled in alongside.

"Go back to the Bar Hook," he told her. "Harry Wilson ought to be back there by now. Tell him to take the best of the two cars and drive like hell to Waterman. I want five more men out here by sunup tomorrow. I want Bud Jeffreys and Crazy Harris—" he named three others he wanted, and four or five alternates in case some were not to be found. All were men he knew, now laid off for the winter at or near Waterman. "Can you remember those?"

"Sure."

"When you've put Harry Wilson on his way, bring a couple of horses and come back. If your father's there—"

"He isn't."

"If you see a couple of poles that would make a stretcher, bring 'em along—one of the horses can trail 'em like a travois. We'll take the boys to the Bake Pan camp."

"On the way!" Jean whirled her horse.

"Wait! Point out to me where Jim and Billy are."

Jean pointed. The light was failing now; but the long slant of the last sun reflected from the upper peaks of the Maricopas with a clear diffused light, so that objects were still distinct far below upon the plain.

"By the line of that arroyo?"

"No, no! Two hand spans to the west of that."

Kentucky Jones made out now a far-off bottle-shaped dot upon the snow among the other dark dots that were sage and grease-wood; he recognized this as Billy Petersen's fallen horse. He could not see where Jim Humphreys lay. But far off to the southwest he could see the 88 riders.

"There they go," he whispered bitterly.

"One of them tried to turn back and over-ride Jim Humphreys," she said, "but Billy Petersen drove him off. I can't see Lee Bishop down there—guess he hasn't got down the trail yet. I'll be back quick as I can." She turned her horse and was gone in a flurry of hoof-lifted snow.

Kentucky Jones took the Bake Pan trail, his horse sliding downward on braced feet as he cut the corners of the switch-back trail.

Lee Bishop was twenty minutes ahead of Kentucky Jones in reaching Billy Petersen and Jim Humphreys; but he had sighted Kentucky on the down trail, and he waited now for Kentucky to come up. Had Lee Bishop not been there, Kentucky might well have overridden his mark, so well did the thickening dusk combine with the sparse scatter of the Bake Pan brush to conceal the dead horse and the man who sat against it.

"They got Jim Humphreys," said Lee Bishop morosely as Kentucky pulled up. "If that boy was shot once he was shot half a dozen times."

"What about Billy!"

Billy Petersen was leaning against his dead horse, his

legs stretched upon his folded saddle blanket. In the failing light his face looked a pale grey-green. "I'm all right," he said without conviction.

"He busted his ankle, some way, when his horse flopped. We better take him over to the lower camp, Kentuck—he thinks he can ride all right if we lead along easy. We'll tie Jim Humphreys on your horse, I guess. He's lying over here about a hundred yards."

They traveled the half mile to the Bar Hook Bake Pan camp slowly, Lee Bishop and Kentucky walking and leading the horses. The horse Billy Petersen rode plodded head down, stolidly; but the other upon which they had lashed Jim Humphreys for his last trip in the saddle fidgeted all the way, made uneasy by the unnatural position of its burden.

"How did this thing start?"

"Me and Jim was coming home," Billy Petersen said, "past our southwest well. The 88 had stuck up a kind of a tripod there, like as if to represent a well of their own, and it made us mad. We threw it down. Coming on about a mile farther we run into these four fellers, riding toward us. We seen 'em all the time, but a long way off. Three of 'em was together, and one laying back, when we met up."

"Who were they?" Kentucky asked.

"Three of 'em," Billy Petersen said, "I never knew. They're new fellers that ain't rode for the 88 long. The other feller was Paul Martinez; but he wasn't there for the bother—he was still a couple of furlongs off, coming up at a high lope, when the row broke. They come up in front of us and stopped. One of 'em said, 'Which of you is boss here?' Jim Humphreys said, 'Who the hell wants to know?' One of 'em says, 'I see you threw down our well tripod.' Jim says, 'And what if I did?' Well, one word led to another, and finally one of 'em says, 'Damn you, Bishop—' "

"Bishop?" said Kentucky.

"That's what he called him. Jim didn't bother to tell him different. Then all of a sudden the guns was out."

"Who pulled the first iron?" Kentucky asked.

"Jim did," said Billy Petersen mournfully. "Jim, he fired the first shot. Only he missed. One of the 88 fellers made the quickest draw I ever see or heard tell of. His first shot put Jim out of business, I think. One of 'em took a throw at me, and the other two poured it into Jim as he went down."

Billy Petersen paused and seemed to sway in the saddle so that Kentucky reached his hand out to him; but Billy set his teeth in his cheek and steadied himself. "I'm all right," he said. "I grabbed out my gun and I threw a shot some place, but I don't know where, because right then my damn pony blew up."

"He sure did," said Lee Bishop. "Boy, that bronc unwound!"

"He made two or three pitches," Billy said, "and then he took and run wild with me for two or three hundred yards. I pulled his fool head right back in my lap, but he just run loco, star gazing. I got him turned around—I don't know where I was exactly when all of a sudden he somersaulted. I forget what I was trying to do right then."

"He was charging back into 'em," grunted Lee Bishop,

"that's what he was trying to do."

"Paul Martinez had come up by then, and he was shouting at the other fellers. We threw a few shots back and forth, but I was behind the horse then. Paul Martinez rode over towards where Jim Humphreys fell; I pasted a couple at him, and he went off with the rest. This—this leg sure feels like something happened to it."

They lifted Billy Petersen off his horse and carried him into the one-room log bunk house which, with two good sized corrals and a barn, constituted the Bake Pan camp of the Bar Hook. Kentucky hastily built a fire while Lee Bishop cut off Billy Petersen's boot. "Catch hold of the top of the bunk, Billy," he said at last. A strangling cry broke from Petersen's throat as Lee Bishop seized the injured ankle and suddenly jerked backward with all his weight. "The poor guy fainted," he told Kentucky. "I don't guess I'll bandage this here till we get some hot water."

"I've got water heating on the stove."

"Give me the makings. Say—where did Jean go?"

Kentucky told him briefly what he had done.

"You sure took things on yourself," said Lee Bishop, eyeing him.

"What did you want done different?" asked Kentucky.

"I don't know as I'd have done anything different. I guess you done all right. The old man sure can't keep from fighting now. From here out it's pile into them and pile into them, and pile in again. All I ask is, save me Bill McCord!"

"What do you want to do with Jim Humphreys?"

"Lay the poor guy out in the stable, I guess."

"Jean Ragland is coming down here with three more horses. I better go on back and meet her on the trail. She'll break her neck sure, rounding those horses down that trail in the dark."

"Get going then. When you get back to the house phone to Waterman for the Doc to come out and reset this leg tomorrow."

"O. K."

## CHAPTER ELEVEN

Kentucky met Jean Ragland near the top of the trail. She had cast loose the leads of her two extra horses at the rim of the descent, and was pushing them ahead of her. They stopped and stood waiting in a tangle on the trail as Kentucky came up. "Don't push that stocking-foot black too close," she called to him; "he'll go cutting up the switch-back."

"Let him," said Kentucky; "we won't need the horses now."

Kentucky never forgot the reluctance of that meeting. He could still feel the dead ungainly weight of Jim Humphreys in his arms, and the news that he had to give Jean burdened him heavily. The abrupt, precipitous descent falling away behind him into thickening dark, and the black loom of the driven horses between himself and Jean filling the trail above him, seeming enormously tall with their haunches grotesquely higher than their heads—these things seemed parts of a nightmare.

"How badly are they hurt?" she asked him.

"Jim Humphreys is dead."

She put a hand to her face and he thought that she

swayed in the saddle. He dropped from his horse and went to her, shouldering between the driven ponies. Reaching her stirrup, he took her hand to steady her; for though he could not see her very well in the closing dark, it seemed to him that she had suddenly turned weak and sick. Her hand gripped his and clung; and even through their heavy gloves he detected the tremor of her fingers.

"Is Billy all right?" she asked, her voice faint.

"He broke his ankle when his horse faded; we'll have to get somebody out from Waterman to set it."

Jean drew a deep shuddering breath. "Why do people have to go smashing around, destroying each other?"

"It's bad," he agreed; "nobody likes it any less than I do. But we'll have to go on with it a little way more."

"The sheriff ought to be able to—"

"Billy says himself that Jim Humphreys fired the first shot. Range shootings always come in as self defense. The fight will have to go on. I didn't get anywhere with Bob Elliot today. I told him what I was going to do, and he said come ahead with it; and we left it there."

Jean freed her hand. Her voice was steadier now. "The house was searched again," she told him. "Nothing much is gone."

"Nothing at all?"

"All that seems to be missing is an old .45; it hasn't been out of its holster for two or three years, to my positive knowledge. Haven't you any theory yet, about who keeps ransacking the house?"

"It's mighty hard," he admitted, "not to put a theory to that. But I'm still following Old Man Coffee's way. If one theory is worse than another, it's a theory that covers just part of a case."

He mounted, and they made their way single file up the trail in silence. The loose horses turned and followed them.

He brought his horse abreast of hers as they gained the level footing of the Bench and she turned to him vaguely. "I don't know if I can stand this, Kentucky, if it goes on much longer. Anything is better than this terrible waiting, and mystery, and nobody understanding each other."

"We'll see the beginning of action tomorrow!"

"Kentucky"—her voice was faint with reluctance—"I'm awfully afraid that we won't."

"What do you mean? With those boys that we sent Harry Wilson for," he assured her, "I could stampede half the cattle in the rimrock back where they belong. You'll see us—"

"The boys you wanted aren't coming, Kentucky."

"Didn't you send Harry Wilson to—"

"I sent him; I told him exactly what you told me to tell him; and he went ripping down that crooked road fit to kill himself."

"Then—"

"My father was there, Kentucky. I didn't even know he was there until I had routed Harry Wilson out of the bunk house and started him to town. He came running out when he heard Harry drive out. I told him what had happened down on the Bake Pan. Kentucky, his face lit up as if it had been what he was waiting for. It was the strangest thing. You could see how terrible it was to him;

yet it was as if he came back to himself again, all in a moment. He started to turn and go to his horse that was still standing saddled near the door."

"But if he means to take up the fight—"

"No, Kentucky; all of a sudden he seemed to remember what he had started to ask in the first place— where Harry Wilson was going in the car. Then I told him what I had done, that you told me to do. He stood there, and he seemed to think. And all that hard terrible light went out of his face again. And in the end it all simmered down to just a kind of a show of mean temper. I never saw him go into moods anything like that before Mason died. This terrible thing has done something to us all."

"You mean he didn't want us to send to Waterman for more—"

"He was furious, Kentucky—in a kind of ugly, discouraged way. He wanted to know who you thought you were, sending for men to hire onto his outfit. Of course I hadn't told him yet about selling you my share of the outfit."

"What did you say to him?"

"Kentucky, I kind of lost my temper for a moment," Jean said. "I told him this was the time to fight, if ever he meant to. Kentucky, as I sat on the rim and heard the guns and saw Jim Humphreys keel out of his saddle— oh, I was plenty sick. But something way down inside of me wants to hang onto the range and won't let go. If they fight—I can see we've got to stand our ground."

"You told him that?"

"Not all that—but other things. It was enough. I guess

122

it was too much."

"What did he do?"

"He told me to get in the house and stay there. He said it plenty forceful! I'd give anything in the world to know what's got into him."

Once more Kentucky was forced to think steadily of the reputation for infallibility which Old Man Coffee had earned—as he said—by his theory of having no theories. One theory in particular that was not pretty to look at was trying to force its way into his mind. But once more he put theory down.

"Campo convinced himself," Jean was continuing, "that it would be an irreparable hurt if Waterman—and the rimrock—got the idea that we meant to make gunfight. The upshot of it was that Dad finally jumped into the other car and went ripping down the road to Waterman after Harry Wilson, to countermand your call for men."

"He sure must have worried about that angle of it considerably," said Kentucky, "to be more heated up over that than about what had happened to Billy and Jim."

"Oh, I think he took what had happened to the boys hard enough, too; but he seemed to think that you and Lee Bishop could do everything that anybody could do. He didn't see any need for me to bring more horses down there; I guess he was afraid to have me on that tough rimrock trail at night."

"But you came," Kentucky said.

"I told you I would—and I hadn't told him I wouldn't."

There was a light in the bunk house as they came into

the Bar Hook layout, and Kentucky looked at Jean questioningly.

"I guess Joe St. Marie has come in," Jean said. "He wasn't here when I started out with the horses. Do you feel like explaining what's happened down on the Bake Pan all over again, to him?"

"No," said Kentucky.

"Neither do I," said Jean. "Let's let him stay where he is. I don't understand that boy anyway, very well."

"Does anyone?"

"I doubt it."

Together they rebuilt the fire in the stove and warmed up something to eat. In the press of events neither one of them took sufficient interest in food to remember afterwards what they had had. After they had eaten, Kentucky supposed that Jean would leave him to his own devices, or to turn in; but she lingered in the kitchen, reluctant to be alone. The night was very still; the occasional cracking of the big timbers in the frost sounded like pistol shots. When that house was full of people, light, and warmth, no house could be more friendly, however the rimrock blizzards might howl beyond the sturdy walls. But tonight the house seemed very big, and very empty, to be inhabited by just one slim girl, all alone.

"I don't know but what I'll sleep in the lean-to tonight, here off the kitchen," Kentucky suggested.

"Yes, do," she said instantly. "I don't know what's the matter with me. The night seems so still, and so empty, and so cold . . ."

Jean sat down upon a low blanketed settee that stood

between the stove and the corner wall, and Kentucky came and sat beside her. There were circles under Jean Ragland's eyes; she was beginning at last to show the effects of the strain which the last ten days had placed upon her. But as she turned to look into his face, he learned again that her blue eyes could be deep and unreadable. Jean Ragland's eyes could pull the heart out of a man, without seeming to intend appeal, or to desire it. He wondered what lay deep down within those eyes which could look so silently, so secretively wise.

"Tell me the truth, Kentucky," she said. "You still don't have any theory?"

He slowly shook his head. "It's hard to follow Old Man Coffee's way," he told her. "It's hard not to have many and many a theory before you have any chance of knowing what a thing is about. But I'm still following Old Man Coffee."

"You still think that if you stay here you will—find out?"

"Jean," he said, "do you want me to find out who killed Mason?"

She shot him a curious but untranslatable glance. He thought that she was not going to answer him; but after a moment she said, "Yes."

For no reason that he could name, he wondered instantly if she had lied. "The facts are beginning to add up a little bit now," he said.

"What are you waiting for?" she said. "What's keeping the answer from you?"

He hesitated. She looked so pitifully tired that he could hardly bring himself to bear down upon her now. Yet he knew that he would be unlikely to have as good a chance again to persuade her to tell him what she knew. Already he knew that Lee Bishop was in danger, that Bill McCord had tried to draw Bishop into a fight that would almost certainly have ended Bishop's life; and he was sure that Jim Humphreys had been killed because he had posed as boss—and hence was perhaps taken for Bishop. He had a durable hunch that others were in immediate danger as an aftermath to the killing of Mason. And he sincerely believed that he had no more right to turn away from the trail than a hound dog has the right to swerve or break ground, once he has put down his nose.

"What is holding me up?" he repeated. "You, Jean."

"I?" she said sharply.

He was silent while he got out his tobacco sack and papers, and began the making of a cigarette. "Don't you think," he said, "that it's about time for you to tell me what you know?"

She stared at the stove, but without seeing the stove. "What makes you think I know anything, Kentucky?"

"Because you once had a theory of your own. You didn't take the bullet at the inquest without having a definite reason, a definite theory of this crime."

She said almost inaudibly, "Yes; that's true. But that blew up when Zack Sanders was found dead. I swear to you, Kentucky—my theory is dead—utterly impossible now."

"That isn't the point," he insisted. "The point is that you did have a theory. That theory was based on something. Something that you saw? Or maybe something that you heard, or knew. Now I want you to tell me what that thing was."

She turned toward him, but defensively; and as she met his eyes her own were tormented. "You—I—"

His keen grey gaze fixed her unwaveringly. "I'm not going to let you evade me any more," he said.

Suddenly some resistance within Jean Ragland seemed to break. She swayed against him, and turning, hid her face against his shoulder. She was breathing in long quavering drags; not sobbing, but as if very close to sobs.

For a moment Kentucky Jones sat motionless. Then he flicked his unlighted cigarette into the kindling box and took the girl into his arms, gently, as if she were a weary child.

Her hands clung to him as he drew her into his arms. She said in a small voice, "Hold me tight, Kentucky. The night is so still, so cold. I keep thinking of how Jim Humphreys is lying tonight, down on the Pan." Presently she turned her face upward to him, with closed eyes, and he kissed her. For a moment with her face turned inward toward his shoulder, she pressed her cheek hard against his; so that when she hid her eyes in the hollow of his shoulder again, there was visible upon her cheek a faint color where the unshaved bristle of his jaw had pressed.

They sat there for some time, there in the corner beyond the stove, in silence except for the soft crackling of the embers of the fire. As he sat with the girl in his arms the coldness and the bleak sense of disaster seemed to go out of the night, and the quiet lost its hostility. That brief hour in which he felt against his body the faint beating of her heart seemed illimitably precious; as if he were here serving as a utility for a little while in a destiny immeasurably beyond and above his own.

Yet he had no illusions concerning the part he was playing here. He believed, as definitely as he had ever believed anything in his life, that she had put herself in his arms as a last resort—silencing his questions in this way when she could no longer otherwise evade him. But some grim factor within him humbly bowed its head, waiting for a different day.

Jean stirred at last, and freed herself lazily from his arms. She smiled at him faintly, her eyes dreamy, misty with sleepiness. "I'm dead for sleep," she told him; "I think I can sleep now—better than I have been, these nights."

He let her go, and when she was gone he smoked his postponed cigarette in a curiously mixed mood, half softened, half grimly ironic. Presently he went to Zack Sanders' bunk, and lying down without taking off his clothes, was almost immediately asleep.

## CHAPTER TWELVE

Not more than half an hour could have passed when he was jerked broad awake by a fluttering knock upon his door. Before he could answer it, the door opened half hurriedly, half in stealth, and Jean's whisper came to him through the dark. "Kentucky, are you there?"

"Here, Jean." He jerked a match out of his pocket and struck it into flame with his thumb nail.

As he stood up she came close to him, her eyes very

big and dark in her pale face. She was wrapped in a brushed wool robe of a red and white Navajo pattern, so much too big for her that it was more like a blanket than a garment. Its ill-fitting folds lay open at her neck, revealing white shoulders and flimsy silk. And about her shoulders bushed the magnificent mass of her fine-spun hair, its color a smoky red-gold in the flare of the match. She was wearing moccasins, and without the high heels of her riding boots she looked less tall than he was accustomed to think of her, and somehow infinitely softer and more easily hurt.

"Jean—what is it?"

"Kentucky—somebody is walking all around us—just as quietly as—one of Joe St. Marie's ghosts."

The hurried phrasing gave him a queer turn for a moment as if she could see things that he could not. "All around us? What do you mean?"

"I mean around the layout here—near the house."

"How many of them?"

"I only saw one. He was prowling through the shadows—I saw him plainly, not more than ten horse jumps away. I couldn't hear a sound he made, even in all this quiet."

"Did it look like anybody you know?"

"I couldn't tell. He was carrying something on his shoulders. Then I thought I heard a walking horse."

"Where did you see this?"

"From the window of my room. I couldn't stand it alone there any more. Sometimes I think I'm going crazy."

"Let's have a look." Kentucky picked up his gun belt.

"Be quiet," she cautioned him. "Whoever it is doesn't want to be seen—that's certain. If we're going to find out who it is, he mustn't know that he's been seen."

"O. K."

She groped for his hand and led the way through the cold dark of the long ranch house.

Jean's room was a small square one in the farther corner, somehow not as big nor as commodious as he had expected. It had two windows, one of which was wide open, so that the room was as frostily cold as the outdoors. At this window she knelt, peering out into the snow-reflected starlight, and he dropped to one knee beside her.

"I first saw him from my bed," she whispered. "He went behind that dwarfed spruce. For a while he stood there behind it—as if he was watching the house. Then he went on, walking as quietly as—as nothing human. As he went out of sight I got up and came to the window; and I watched him until I couldn't see him any more. He went toward the pump house, and out of sight."

"I don't see any sign of him now."

Jean seized his arm, and he heard her breath in her teeth. "What's that? There, close in the shadow of the pump house?"

Kentucky looked hard where she pointed. He could not at once be sure whether he saw anything or not; but as he stared, straining his eyes against the bad light, he presently began to believe that he could make out the crouching figure of a man.

It produces a queer sensation to study a shadow in the semblance of a man who crouches, watching, for an unknown purpose in the dark. For half a minute, as he stared trying to make certain of that halfseen figure, Kentucky forgot the girl at his side altogether; but he remembered her abruptly as he realized that she was shivering with uncertainty and the cold. "Get into your bed," he whispered. "I'll watch here."

She shook her head. Her eyes were fixed with a frozen fascination upon the shadow which seemed to conceal the figure of a watcher. Kentucky put an arm about her, and as he drew her against his side he could feel the cold tremors that ran the whole length of her body.

For what seemed a long time they knelt there, their eyes fixed upon the shadow against the pump house. Once Kentucky was certain that he not only perceived the whole outline of the crouched figure, but had seen it move; and his hand moved toward his gun. But the shadow blurred and lost outline again, and he waited, unsure.

When the telephone broke into abrupt outcry in the house behind them the sudden burst of sound struck across their tense nerves like the crack of a whip against fiddle strings. Jean jerked violently; then, pulling herself together, whispered, "Damn!" The telephone continued to ring.

Kentucky whispered, "One of us will have to answer that. I think you'd better go. I'll stay and watch the shadow here. If it's for me, please take the message."

Jean Ragland hesitated, then silently obeyed. With his eyes riveted upon their mark, Kentucky listened for what seemed a long time to the low murmur of Jean's voice, two rooms away.

Presently, alone, and with his eyes accustomed to their work, he saw the secret of the mysterious shadow dissolve, so that he finally recognized it for what it was—a bush, a wagon spring, and a broken buckboard wheel. Whomever Jean had seen prowl the layout, and wherever he might be now, he was no longer in the shadow of the pump house—and had not been, since they had watched that shadow together.

Disgusted, Kentucky rose, straightening his cramped knees. One long step from the window stood Jean Ragland's bed. He could see almost as much of the terrain from its edge as he could from the sill, and he now sat down upon it, careful to avoid a creaking of the springs.

Her bed was still warm to his hand, where Jean had lain and tried to sleep; and for a moment he marveled that the toss of circumstances should have brought him so near to this girl, even for so little time. Then—he noticed something else.

Something was wrong with the mattress upon which he sat. Unmistakably, there was something within that mattress that had nothing to do with sleep. Suddenly Kentucky dropped to one knee beside the bed and thrust his hand between the mattress and the sheet.

Buried in the mattress his fingers found the polished wood of a rifle stock; and beside it, dismounted, the cool smooth steel of the barrel. For a moment his hand rested on these while something turned over in the pit of his stomach and refused to go back into place. He withdrew his hand, and sat down limply on the edge of the bed. He was not ready to say what the discovery meant; but he knew instantly that Jean was more deeply involved than he had supposed—perhaps far more deeply. "Dear God," he whispered, "what have we here? What have we here?"

The murmur of Jean's voice within the house had ceased; and though he did not hear her moccasins, he heard the faint stir of the door as she came into the room. He stood up, overwhelmed with such pity for this ill-situationed girl that he was the victim of an unaccustomed timidity. She came close to him and her hand touched his arm.

"That shadow was a misdeal," he whispered. "There isn't anybody in that shadow. I don't believe there's anybody out there any more." She said, "Oh."

He felt infinitely gentle toward her, and compassionate. Presently he knew that he would have to ask her why that gun was concealed in her mattress. He was unable to ask her yet. "What was the phone call?" he asked.

"That was for you," she told him. "I've always heard that that insane old man didn't know night from day; but wouldn't you think he'd have enough sense not to—"

"Who was it?"

"It was Mark Ferris, that gunsmith at Waterman. He's still trying to trace Zack Sanders' gun for you."

"Yes? Quick! What did he say?"

"He said—" Jean was shivering so violently that she could hardly control the chattering of her teeth.

"Wait a minute." Kentucky picked her up, sweeping her off her feet with an arm under her knees, and laid her on the open bed; then pulled the blankets over her, and pressed the edges close about her throat. "Now go on," he said.

"He said that he got to thinking that maybe you'd made a mistake in reading the number you wanted traced. He started looking through his records again on the idea that you might have mistaken an 8 for a 3. He thinks now that that is what you did; because he has a record of such a gun, except that the serial number begins with 8. He's sure that this is the gun you meant. He sold it secondhand about a year ago."

"In God's name, woman, who did he sell it to?"

"To Joe St. Marie."

For perhaps half a moment Kentucky Jones was completely still. Then he sucked in a deep breath and began to swear through his teeth with the vicious intonation of a man who puts his whole heart into it. He had suddenly become aware that he had perhaps put off the formation of one theory for a little bit too long.

Suddenly he whirled to the window, crouched low to avoid the sash, and vaulted the sill. He heard Jean speak his name behind him, but he was racing for the bunk house. A match was already in his hand as he thrust open the door; he struck it on the logs and with quick efficient motions lighted one of the hanging lamps.

"St. Marie—" he said aloud.

Joe St. Marie's bunk was empty. The bronc rider's bed-roll was gone, and the slenderly made, silver-mounted bridle of Indian workmanship which he had always kept hanging at the head of his bunk. Kentucky swore again, blew out the light, and left the bunk house on the dead run. He headed now for the corral nearest the pump house, and sprang half way up the corral fence.

The half dozen horses in the corral were huddled together near the empty feed box. The ponies moved and shifted, but by the time he had counted them Kentucky knew which horse was gone. This information only verified, however, what Kentucky had already guessed. Joe St. Marie, leaving stealthily, as Kentucky now knew Jean had seen him leave, was certain to take the best-conditioned horse upon the place, in this case a raw-boned claybank. There were doubtless other horses under the Bar Hook brand which would out-travel the big claybank, but assuredly none of them were in the corrals that night. Kentucky leaned against the fence and pressed the palms of his hands against his eyes. He was picturing to himself the lay of the country, and the probable intricacies of Joe St. Marie's mind. Immediately he came to a conclusion which he had no reason to be certain was sound, but which was the best he could form from what information he had.

Once more he drove through the clogging snow at a run, this time to the house; here he got his hat and his coat, his gloves and his spurs. After that he went to the stable for his saddle and rope, and without hesitation put a loop upon the pony which he believed would come the nearest to matching the claybank's performance tonight—a wiry, almost under-sized steel-dust pony, strong with the markings of Indian blood. The pony was salty with the cold, and nervous with the haste of Kentucky's movements; but Kentucky already had the blanket on and was swinging his fifty-pound saddle aboard by the horn as Jean, coming out from the house, reached his side.

"What—where are you going? What's happened?"

A sudden crazy anger came into Kentucky, like a stroke of white lightning. At its impact all the compassion, all the tenderness he had felt for this girl seemed to vanish, as if she held him under a hypnosis, the spell of which had snapped. He turned on her furiously.

"What is it to you where I go or what I do? Men put their hands in the lion's mouth for you, and you tell them nothing—not even enough so that they can take care of their own lives!"

She stared at him a moment in utter bewilderment, and one hand went to her throat. "Why, Kentucky—why, Kentucky—I've told you more—more than—"

He said, "You trust no one, you work with no one; everyone trusts you, and you let us all ride blind."

He turned furiously to his horse and drew the latigo up with a snap that jerked a grunt out of the animal. And he set his teeth in his lip lest he utter the belief which had overwhelmed him: that Jim Humphreys had died because of the reticence of this slim girl, now standing beside him in the snow.

"But—but—" Jean Ragland's eyes looked enormous in her white face. The loose mass of her hair, lifted sideways by the frozen wind off the Maricopas, seemed to quiver as it yielded to the stir of the air. She shivered; the untrampled snow beyond the corral poles was no whiter than her blue-veined ankles, or her knuckles as she held the robe close at her throat. And though she was a tall girl, Kentucky Jones loomed above her like a tree, so that even then in his anger he saw that she was a pitiful and desolated figure. Yet he was seeing Jim Humphreys' face as he had seen it last, staring with unseeing eyes at the first stars; and, believing that Jim Humphreys' death could have been prevented, had Kentucky known what this girl must know, he could not forgive her. His low, uncompromising voice cut hers down.

"I've been taken for a fool and used as a fool," he said. "But I tell you this: I'm going to ride this thing out. I'm going to ride this thing clear through to the end, regardless of what the end is. You hear me? And when that's done I'm through."

Jean Ragland's face contorted tragically, exactly as if he had cut her with his quirt. One of her hands faltered to her mouth, and her teeth closed on a knuckle. She managed to say, "What are you going to do?"

"I'm going to try to cut off St. Marie at Hightman's Gap. If I don't get him there, I may or may not go on. I haven't decided yet."

"You think—you think he—"

"The man who put the gun into Zack's hand is the man responsible for his death, just as surely as if he shot Zack himself and that gun was St. Marie's. I'm going to have me that man. When I've got him, I'm going to turn and get me the man that killed Mason. And I don't care who it is, or how close to home, or if it splits the rimrock wide open when he's caught."

It had been on his tongue to tell her that she might shield whom she wanted to, lie to whom she wanted to, conceal what evidence she wanted to, but he would see the killer of Mason hung in the end; but he bit this back.

Still jerky and explosive with his anger, he vaulted into the saddle.

The pony was cold and stiff, and should have been warmed up gradually; but Kentucky Jones was not thinking about the care of ponies. He poured in quirt and spur with savage disregard, and at the corral gate jumped the pony over the two lower bars, which he had not stopped to throw down.

He did not look back; but as he slammed out of the Bar Hook layout, he somehow knew that she was still standing there in the snow, stopping her mouth with her knuckles as she watched him as far as he could be seen. And he wondered if it was impossible for this girl to go to pieces, like other women, and lose herself in tears.

## CHAPTER THIRTEEN

As the buildings of the Bar Hook dropped behind him, presently becoming no more than a dark irregularity on the vast sweep of the Bench, the anger went out of him; and with the anger the heart seemed to go out of him also, leaving him weak, and entirely reckless of what might happen next. His horse was already blowing hard from the cold start he had given it. He pulled it down to a shuffling trot and pointed up-country across long broken reaches of snow.

For four miles he held steadily northward, then turned and swung a broad circle, seeking to cut a trail which would verify the supposed direction of St. Marie. Four times he crossed promising trails, but each, when he dismounted to examine it, proved to be old. He was far to the eastward when he at last cut a straight-drawn track made within the hour. He judged that the bronc rider was pushing northeast at a cat-trot, trying—as Jones had guessed—for Hightman's Gap.

He knew that St. Marie, once aware that he was followed, would never permit himself to be overtaken from behind. Kentucky was only half familiar with the Wolf Bench terrain, but he concluded that he would have to try to come upon Hightman's Gap by a different way, even at the risk of not coming upon it at all. He turned north, leaving St. Marie's trail, and pressed up-country at a hammering trot.

The trail he was making looped across Wolf Bench at a long slant, first over long reaches of the faintly rising and falling open country of the Bench, then more deeply into a country of boulders and thin-scattered timber. Sometimes the deep impassable gashes that laced the Bench outguessed him so that he had to go a long way around; and when this happened he had to push his horse harder than he had allowed for, to make up for the distance and time he had lost. But the steel-dust pony was a good mountain animal, a horse bred to the rimrock; it adjusted itself to the treachery of the unseen footing under the snow with almost the surety of the dainty-footed, cat-climbing mules of the Maricopa pack trails.

The hours passed and the pony tired, and it seemed to Kentucky Jones that that ride was perhaps the longest and loneliest he had ever made in his life. He could not keep Jean Ragland out of his mind. Over and over she returned to him with a reality more sharp and inescapable than as if she had been riding at his side.

He remembered the strong sharp pressure of her fingers, and the touch of her cheek, and the pliant, yielding curve of her body in his arms; he could see the stir and drift of her loose hair as they had stood in the corral, and the impelling, unnamed emotion in her eyes as she had stood staring at him with her knuckle between her teeth; and he could smell the clean touch of frost upon brushed wool. This girl had become the center of all living, as a waterhole is the center of a range, or a fire the center of a camp. He had never been called upon to admit this to himself, until suddenly circumstances had asked him to accept also the certainty that she had betrayed them all.

For he could not avoid recognition that Jean's concealment of the rifle had a different meaning than had that extraordinary feat of hers at the inquest, when she had lifted the bullet that killed Mason from under the very nose of the sheriff. Her concern with the bullet had told him that she was shielding someone—if not the killer, then at least someone who might otherwise have been open to an unfair suspicion. Although, in the case of the bullet, she had availed herself of his help, he had been able to understand that he remained an outsider here, who could not expect to be told in what sort of thing he had assisted her. But in spite of Old Man Coffee he had assumed that she was at least cooperating with the interest of her father and her father's brand.

But the discovery of the hidden rifle told him at once that she was cooperating with no one; that, incredibly, she was playing an utterly lone hand—at least, he reflected bitterly, as far as the Bar Hook was concerned. For certainly no man had had anything to do with hiding a rifle in a bed. A man, and particularly a cowman, who sought to hide something would hide it by means of distance and inaccessibility; the bottom of a waterhole in some far cienega would have been the ultimate resting place of the undesirable rifle. In this vast broken country only a woman would select a cache so close under the light.

She was acting, then, without cooperation with her father, or any other of the Bar Hook personnel. The association of this fact with the circumstances of Jean's rendezvous with her father's enemy was unavoidable.

To this unhappy situation the revelation of St. Marie's connection added a sharp immediacy. He believed now that the materials for solution had been under their hands; and were now perhaps lost to them because Jean had concealed the very signs that would have shown the trail. Because of her concealment of evidence, the Bar Hook had moved uncertainly, helpless in the dark; and the result was that a good tall boy was dead, and others would perhaps join him before it was through.

In his present state of disillusionment and the dregs of anger, he was supported by no particle of faith. He could not put her out of his mind. But she seemed to him to be like a mirage, which lures all the sanity out of a thirsty man, yet contains nothing of honesty, nor sincerity, nor faithfulness, when finally it is reached.

He pushed on steadily, counting upon the toughness of his pony. By the stars he knew that his general direction was true; but he had made so many detours that he no longer had any idea of how far he had come, or whether he could reach the trail into Hightman's Gap that night or not. His hope that he would be able to make it before

St. Marie was very like a prayer. Until now the smash of six-guns had never been associated in his mind with anything more desirable than the raw, sickly smell of blood. But now, for once in his life, he had a stubborn ugly urge to throw bullets into something alive, and blow it off the face of the earth. He hoped fervently not only that he would head Joe St. Marie, but that St. Marie would fight.

Then, unexpectedly, he found that he was in country that he knew; and in three hundred yards more he recognized the trail into Hightman's Gap. A faint persistent whisper of wind in the scrub oak and juniper concealed from him the sound of any movement upon the trail. He approached with caution, stopped his horse and swung deep out of the saddle, not daring to set foot to the ground. There had been riders through that gap since the snow, perhaps half a dozen in either direction: carefully, with ungloved hand, he explored a section of the trail inch by inch, until he was satisfied that no man had passed this way before him in the last twenty-four hours.

He crossed the trail and guided his horse in an aimless parallel for a little way, to simulate the trail of a loose horse wandering the range. Then he proceeded into the gap, ice crackling under foot where the snow had been crushed by passing hoofs. Twice he stopped to listen, but heard no approach; and so came at last to a place which he thought would serve his purpose. He turned his horse up a slope so precipitous that his pony came down on one knee in the second stride; and a little way above the trail, in a twisted bunch of junipers, found cover sufficient for a man and a horse. By daylight it would not have served, but in the deep shadow of the gap, with only the thin light of the stars to moderate the dark, it was enough.

The steel-dust pony found a level place to put its feet, and stood with hoofs bunched and head down, well worn out. Its long slow breaths drifted down wind slowly on the still air, faintly visible for a moment before they vanished. Kentucky Jones brushed the snow off a bit of rock, rolled himself a cigarette, and listened to the quiet.

He had time for a second cigarette, and a third, leisurely smoked, with long waits between. He presently began to think that he had misread Joe St. Marie's purpose, and that the man had taken some other way. But there was nothing to do but wait, his brain tired out with its own running, like the horse. Somewhere afar off a pair of coyotes called and answered. He heard the distant hoot of a great owl, like the grunt of something enormous and uncanny, such as never existed on mountain or plain. And once, far off, he heard a rush of slipping snow where something stealthy for a moment moved carelessly, or in fear.

When at last he heard an approaching horse it startled him, it had come so close before he heard it at all. For a little while he could make out no creak of leather, so that he feared the animal was not ridden; but presently the hurried tempo of the running walk at which the animal came on assured him that it was a ridden horse. He rose cautiously, freed his gun in its leather and put his left arm around the pony's head to hold down its nose, preventing its whinny to the stranger.

Around a shoulder of rock seventy-five yards away the

rider appeared; and he recognized the broad-banded black and white Mackinaw that Joe St. Marie wore.

Kentucky Jones could see now why he had been so late in hearing St. Marie's approach. St. Marie was riding not in the center of the trail but in the rougher going at the side, avoiding the ice formed by the hoof-crushed snow in the trail itself. Even then, Kentucky had a moment of admiration for the horsemanship of this man. Under Joe St. Marie's saddle the sleepiest old plug always looked alertly awake, and spoiled horses, with mouths tougher to the bit than the grip of a man's hand, took on an unexpectedly decent sensitivity. It was as if something about St. Marie put into horses the fear of God.

Kentucky's horse stirred and blew out its breath, anxious to signal the other horse. St. Marie was now within the twenty-five yards; he was leaning a little sideways in the saddle, peering into the junipers so directly that Kentucky thought the bronc rider was looking him straight in the face. Yet St. Marie came on. Kentucky drew his gun, and waited until St. Marie was almost below him.

His voice was low as he spoke, but coming unexpectedly out of the quiet from within ten yards it lifted St. Marie like a fired gun. "Just a minute, Joe!"

The result was as if Kentucky had snapped a strip of hide from St. Marie's horse with a bull whip. The animal snorted and went forward in a great bound as St. Marie's spurs struck. Joe St. Marie himself in the same instant flung himself half out of the saddle and behind his horse. He had hooked his spur on the side nearest Kentucky into the cantle of his saddle and was riding low on the far stirrup, but the effect from where Kentucky stood was as if he had disappeared.

Kentucky's horse, startled by the other's stampede, half freed itself with a great stamping of feet, throwing Kentucky off balance as he fired; but the shot caught St. Marie's horse in its third jump. As the gun spoke the horse went down on its knees, nose into the snow, as if it had hit the end of a rope. Its hind quarters whipped upward and for a moment it seemed to hesitate, pivoting on the curve of its neck; then it slammed down upon its side.

Kentucky was already down into the trail. Behind him his horse went down in a great thrashing of hoofs and tearing of juniper, thrown by the tied reins as it tried to stampede. Kentucky, gun in hand, sprang across St. Marie's downed horse to where the rider lay.

St. Marie lay on his back, his hands above his head, one of them still holding his gun, cocked but unfired. Kentucky took the gun with his left hand. He would have eased the hammer down, but St. Marie's horse, shot through the shoulders, was trying to get up, straining its neck toward its withers. Using St. Marie's gun, Kentucky put a bullet through its head.

The bronc rider was breathing heavily, but except that he had been knocked out by the throw, Kentucky could not find anything wrong with him. When he had satisfied himself that St. Marie had no other weapon of any account, he unfastened St. Marie's bed-roll from the fallen horse, kicked it out flat, and dragged St. Marie onto it. Then he sat down on the horse to await results.

He studied the knocked-out man with a curious impartiality. This bronc rider was a man of a peculiarly mixed type. In all things he was a figure distinct and complete in himself, with no ambition whatever to be anything that he was not; and he was a rider who could do more with a horse than any other man. But here an element of essential worthlessness stepped in. Fast and efficient though he might be while he worked, no boss could be sure St. Marie was at work at all, once he was out of sight.

St. Marie groaned, and swore faintly in Spanish. But it was a quarter of an hour more before St. Marie at last propped himself up on an elbow and looked at Kentucky with comprehension. Kentucky saw the bronc rider stealthily ascertain that he was no longer armed.

"Go ahead," Kentucky said, reading his mind, "pick up a rock. But when you do I'm going to blow your arm right off at the wrist."

"Where's my mouth organ?"

"Never mind the mouth organ. I didn't come up here for a concert."

St. Marie sat up and rubbed his head with both hands. He looked around for his hat, recovered it, and tried to put it on; but flinched, and left it perched at a drunken angle on the side of his head. Once more he stared at Kentucky Jones.

Kentucky smoked, and idly twirled his gun by the trigger guard; but he did not open conversation. He wanted St. Marie to begin that.

"I suppose," said St. Marie at last, "you're waiting for the others to come up."

"There aren't any others."

"What are you waiting for then?"

"I'm waiting for you to talk."

"I got nothing to say."

"If you don't want to talk," said Kentucky, "I'm not a damn bit interested in trying to make you. Just keep your mouth shut tight enough and long enough and you're through—and that suits me."

St. Marie studied him again. "Listen," he said at last, "listen. You guys got no call to rub me out. It'll only make it worse for you in the end—Campo ought to know that. Just as likely as not, gunning me will be the one thing that turns around and hangs all the rest of it on him, before he's through."

"You're mixed up," Kentucky grunted. "I've got no doubt you'll be rubbed out all right. But it won't be here or now, and it won't be by me. You're going up the chimney by due process of law, Joe."

St. Marie seemed mystified. "You think you're having a lot of fun with me, don't you?" he said at last. "But don't you think for a minute that I don't know what you're here for, and why you were sent, just as well as you do."

"I guess you're some affected by that knock on the head," Kentucky told him.

St. Marie leaned forward, hitching nearer Kentucky. "Listen—"

"Stay where you are," Kentucky warned him.

"All right. I'm not trying anything funny. Listen—who's with you?"

"How many of me do you think it takes to take you where you're going?"

147

The quarter-blood seemed to take a flying grip on hope. "Look here," he said. "Look here! Campo Ragland's got me wrong. I know you don't know me very good—but *Nombre de Dios,* Kentuck—I swear before God I'm telling you the truth. I've shot square with Campo all along, and all the way. He's got no more reason to send you to get me, than as if he sent me to get you."

"You're trying to whip over the skyline on us, aren't you?"

"And what if I am? Wouldn't you? Listen, Kentucky—if I hadn't meant to shoot square with Campo Ragland, do you think I'd have stayed at the Bar Hook as long as I did? And I'd have stuck with him right on through it, too; I'd have backed his play any way he wanted. Yes, by God, I will yet! Campo Ragland had no call on earth to be afraid of me."

"Afraid of you?" Kentucky repeated.

"That's what's gone haywire with that Godforsaken outfit," St. Marie said. In the lack of light his face showed only as a dusky blur. But there was a fanatic intensity in the stare which he held upon Kentucky's face. "That man has gone to pieces," he insisted. "That man isn't right any more. I wouldn't have left the Bar Hook at all, only pretty soon I seen that Campo was getting scared, and scared of me. That man is crazy."

"You're spinning somewhat yourself," said Kentucky, "if you think that Campo Ragland is afraid of any bronc rider that walks."

"That man has gone to pieces," St. Marie reiterated. Kentucky perceived that the man believed himself to be

148

talking for his life. "Nobody that knows anything about this is safe in the same county with him any more. Maybe you're not safe yourself, for all you know. But look, Kentucky, I swear to God Ragland had no call to worry about me, even if I stayed in the rimrock; and he has a thousand times less reason to put me out of business, and head me off from what I'm trying to do now— or was trying to do, when you shot my horse out from under me."

"And just what is this you're trying to do?"

"All I want is to get out of this country. Where I made my mistake, I was saving the damn horse. I should have pushed through this here gap two hours ago. *Jesu!* All I want of this business is out."

"I expect you do," said Kentucky. "But you're too deep in this business, Joe."

"What difference does it make how deep I'm in, so long as I can keep my mouth shut, and disappear out of here? I—"

"A lot of difference," Kentucky told him. "I damn well mean to take you back."

St. Marie appeared to be dumbfounded. "Take me back?" he repeated.

"What did you think I was going to do, murder you?"

St. Marie stared at him again. "Yeh," he said at last.

Kentucky rolled a cigarette and considered. "We don't seem to see eye to eye in this, St. Marie," he said. "In the first place, I wasn't sent after you by Campo Ragland. Campo doesn't even know you've left the Bar Hook— so far as I know."

There was a considerable pause. "Jones," St. Marie

149

said at last, "who are you? Are you a government man?"

"No," said Kentucky. "I've come out here to take you back on my own hook."

"In God's name what for?"

"I guess," said Kentucky, "I'll ask you a couple of questions for a change."

St. Marie shivered, but appeared to take heart. "And what if I give you the wrong answers?" he said.

"Then," said Kentucky, "I suppose you'll go right ahead and hang. Don't let me stop you."

"Hang? For what?"

"For the killing of Zack Sanders."

For an instant St. Marie did not move. Then he drew a deep breath and let it go again. "I sure as hell don't know what you're talking about," he said. "Give me a cigarette."

Kentucky tossed him the makings. "I'm going to describe a gun to you," he said. "The gun I'm thinking of is a blue-barreled .45. It has a hard rubber grip on the left side, but the grip on the other side got broke and was replaced with a piece of cigar box whittled to fit. There's a little piece split off the wooden part of the grip. The serial number looks like it begins with a 3, but it's really an 8." Kentucky told him the rest of the number.

"That's my gun," said St. Marie. "Or anyway, it was my gun once."

"I know that," said Kentucky. "I found that out from the gunsmith in Waterman. Now I want to know exactly when and why you shoved that gun into the hand of Zack Sanders."

"I never did give it to Zack Sanders," said St. Marie.

Kentucky Jones lost patience. "Get yourself ready to walk," he said. "I got no time to listen to you lie!"

"Tell me just this one thing," St. Marie pleaded. "Where did you get track of this gun?"

"The gun we're talking about," Kentucky said, "was in Zack Sanders' hand as he lay dead near the Bar Hook pump house."

The bronc rider swore softly. "If you're trying to hook me into something by way of that," he said, "you're up the wrong coulee. I lost that gun in a crap game in Waterman four months back. I can name you every man that was in that crap game, and they'll swear to what I say; and Ted Baylor will tell you that gun is the one he won from me that night."

"Ted Baylor in a crap game with a bunch of saddle bums? That's a hot one!"

"He was drunk, and he just stopped for one pass as he went through," Joe St. Marie insisted. "The lucky stiff got my gun on that one pass."

"If that's so," Kentucky said, "that can be checked up later. For the time being I'm taking you back."

"If you aim to take me back, I can just as well kiss myself good-by right now. I ain't got a Chinaman's chance of living to see trial—and well you know it! I thought you swung with Campo Ragland. I even thought you were thick with Ragland's girl. You sure had me fooled."

"What makes you think I don't swing with Ragland?"

"If you swung with the Bar Hook, the last thing you'd want to do would be to drag me back into this case."

"Then come clean and come quick—I'm cold, and I'm

stiff, and I'm ready to ride!"

The bronc rider was beginning to crack under the strain. "I don't know what your side is," he said hoarsely, "nor who you think you're working for, or why. But if you're fool enough to think you're helping out Campo Ragland, you're making one hell of a blunder."

"Answer me this," said Kentucky, "and if I figure you've answered me with a lie, we're going to start back right now without any more talk. What do you know about the killing of Sanders?"

"I swear I never knew Zack Sanders was dead until Lee found him," St. Marie said passionately.

"Then tell me this," said Kentucky again. "You saw the killing of Mason?"

"No," said St. Marie violently. "No! I wasn't anywhere near it."

"It's pretty well known," said Kentucky, "that you weren't where you were supposed to be that day."

"What if I wasn't? That Campo is a driving fool. I figured I'd done enough work for one week, and I took me a layoff on my own hook. Any cowboy does that when he thinks he's worked enough—or anyway they do where I come from."

"And where were you when you saw the shooting of Mason?"

"I never seen it, I tell you! I was riding in, but I was anyway half a mile off and beyond the ridge when I heard the shots. I didn't even suspicion anything then. I went up to the house for grub. All in God's world I ever seen, when I went by the kitchen window Campo

152

Ragland was cleaning his gun, his deer rifle. I never even knew Mason was dead until Lee Bishop found him that night. And I never knew that deer rifle killed him until the sheriff come out to see about Zack Sanders' killing, and told us Mason was killed by a small caliber. I swear—"

"You recognized the caliber of the gun he was cleaning as you walked past the window?"

"I went on in the kitchen. He'd put it away from him by then. It was clear over on the other side of the room. But it was the only rifle in the room, and I knew that that was the one he'd had in his hands. I—"

"How come you to take such close notice of what was the caliber of the gun standing against the wall?"

"How can a feller help knowing the different guns around a place by sight? I've used that gun myself."

Kentucky Jones said slowly, "Was there anybody else at the ranch house then?"

"Campo's girl was there. She was in the kitchen talking to her father. They'd been having a fight about something. But they cut it off quick when I come in. The girl looked like she wasn't feeling so good."

Kentucky leaned forward, and his voice sounded as if it could saw chunks out of the frozen rock. "St. Marie, is that all you know?"

"All I know?" His voice rose in insolent revolt. "What the hell do you think—" He checked. Kentucky Jones had cocked his gun, and the small metallic click tamed the bronc rider more effectively than as if Kentucky had downed him with a rock. "*Jesu*, Kentuck," he cried. "I can't tell you anything more! *Sangre!* It's enough to get my head shot off as it is!"

"You're giving me this as the whole reason for stealing a horse and going over the hill tonight?"

"In God's name, why wouldn't I go over the hill? Here's Campo with a killing on his hands that's stirred up the rimrock like no killing ever stirred it up before. Here's me, maybe the only man that knows a thing that would hang Campo higher than a buzzard. Is that reason for going over the hill or not? But I tell you I'd have stayed through if I hadn't seen him going to pieces right in front of my eyes! When fear comes into a man nobody's safe."

"I'd give a thousand dollars," said Kentucky, "to know if you're telling the truth."

For a moment Joe St. Marie dropped his gesticulating hands and said nothing. Then suddenly—"Give me my saddle," he babbled, "and let me go! I can keep my mouth shut, I tell you! I can forget I ever worked for the Bar Hook! I can forget I ever set eyes on the rim! Let me get out of this God-forsaken country and you'll—"

"For God's sake shut up!" said Kentucky. He was feeling not less than two thousand years old, and very weary of the world. But he did not hesitate over his decision. "Have you got any money?" he said in a dead voice.

"No."

"Take your saddle on your back," he told St. Marie. "How far is it to the nearest place where a man can borrow a horse?"

"Nine—eleven miles."

"Take your saddle on your back and walk. And your

bed-roll too. Borrow you a horse. See that that horse dies running—and never let me set eyes on you again."

For a moment St. Marie sagged, the steam taken out of him by the sudden realization that he had got out of his box. But true to that dark strain in his blood, he had no word of thanks, no word for his luck; his next remark was in the form of a complaint.

"I can't walk all that," he said. "That's a long day's walk. And carrying a saddle and a bed-roll—"

"You've got better than two hours before morning," said Kentucky. "You'll borrow that horse as the sun comes up. Have they got a phone there?"

"No."

"Good."

"But look—if they ever catch up with me they'll have me back here for horse stealing."

"Yes," said Kentucky. "I wouldn't trust you loose if I didn't know there'd be hell on your heels as you go." Kentucky pulled off his gloves and looked through his pockets. He found six dollars in silver cart wheels, and tossed them onto St. Marie's blanket. "I've got just one more thing to say to you," he said. "If ever I see you in this country again—go for your iron, because I'm going to gun you down. And if ever Campo Ragland is tried for murder, no matter on whose say-so—even if you've kept your mouth shut—I'll hunt you down if it takes a lifetime. You hear me?"

"You'll have to come deep into Sonora," said St. Marie, "if you want to see me again."

"I don't. Help me get this horse off the trail. That bullet through his withers is going to make him draw unfavorable notice, if he's found."

Kentucky got the steel-dust pony; he put his lassrope on the dead horse, and with the assistance of Joe St. Marie on foot dragged the carcass to a point from which it could be pitched over a drop, out of sight of the trail until the coyotes had time to do their work.

"Give me my gun," said St. Marie. "I'll have to tell them I broke my horse's leg and had to shoot him—and what will they think if I have no gun?"

"Tell them you had to take your rope and hang him!"

Kentucky wheeled his horse to the trail, and began the long return plod to the Bar Hook; and the first faint greyness of another day was showing at the earth's edge as he came out of Hightman's Gap.

## CHAPTER FOURTEEN

It was noon when Kentucky got back to the Bar Hook. When he had unsaddled and fed his ridden-out pony he lost no time in heading for the kitchen. Here he was wolfing cold meat and equally cold French fried potatoes, washed down with coffee from the pot that always waited on the back of the stove, when Jean found him.

The pallor of fatigue increased the look of fragility that had altered her since the death of Mason; but her self-sufficiency seemed to have returned overnight. Perhaps she had been able to present that illusion to the others all along. For a little while she had allowed Kentucky to see what a blind drift of doubt, fear, perhaps despair, had possessed her; but now the bars were up, shutting him out again.

She said in a flat, incurious voice, "Have a good ride?"

That stopped him for a moment. Last night he had held this girl in his arms—not momentarily, but for what might have been an hour; and later, in a burst of smoking temper, he had left her standing in the snow with tears upon her cheeks. He had ridden all night after a fugitive—perhaps a murderer; she did not know whether he had found the man, or killed him, or what he had learned if St. Marie was taken alive. Yet the indifference of her voice suggested literally that Kentucky might have been the horse he had ridden—or some other horse.

"I rode through mile after mile of buttonhole bushes," he told her, "all blooming in the snow. And it looks as if it might not rain, I hope. Did your father get back?"

"No. He's still in Waterman. So is Harry Wilson. Doc Hopper came out. They've brought Billy up here already."

"The devil! Where is he?"

"Here, I said." Her voice took on a faint edge. "Do you want to see him?"

"In a minute. Where's Lee Bishop?"

"He rode out again."

She stood waiting, watching him without warmth, without dispraise, without any expression whatever. He gulped down the remainder of his coffee in silence. And when he finished she led him to the room where Billy Petersen lay.

Billy Petersen was propped up in a four-poster bed that must have been hauled into the rimrock long ago, in the early days of the brand. It could have belonged to no one but Jean's mother; and the room it occupied was obviously the most favored room in the house. The walls were hung with pictures, and a gayety of hooked rugs and cretonne curtains was augmented in warmth and color by the crackling blaze in the fireplace.

In this environment the unshaved cowboy in the bed looked extraordinarily out of place, as if he not only had been put here against his will, but felt pretty sure that he would be kicked out as soon as the old boss got back. A book, face down in a chair by the bed, told Kentucky that Jean had probably been reading to Billy. Undoubtedly, the youngster was mystified by all this attention. Kentucky, however, was not mystified; the whole thing suggested that Jean had been moved to try to make up to Billy Petersen what could never be made up to Jim Humphreys, who was dead.

"What are you doing up here?" Kentucky demanded. "Doc Hopper should have left you down on the Bake Pan!"

"It wasn't Doc Hopper," Billy told him. "I didn't get no sleep last night. About four o'clock this morning I made Lee saddle up and bring me. About half way I wished I'd stayed where I was. It sure didn't do me no good."

There was a moment's pause while Kentucky Jones waited for the inevitable question about how he had come out with Joe St. Marie. Yet the question did not come; and Kentucky abruptly recognized that Billy Petersen had not been told anything about where Kentucky had gone.

"Do you know where Lee went?" he asked Billy.

"He's gone gunning after Bill McCord."

*"Gunning after—"* Kentucky turned on Jean. "Why

didn't you tell me this as soon as I came in?"

"I didn't know it," she said, the flat indifference of her voice unchanged.

Billy Petersen said, "Lee told me not to say anything about it until he was long gone. I wouldn't say anything now; except I sure don't like this business, Kentuck—I thought maybe you'd want to go and side him, or something."

"Dear God!" Kentucky exploded. "Right into their hands! How long has he been gone?"

"About two hours."

"Was he going straight to the 88?"

"No; I don't guess he was going to the 88 at all. He figured he'd go over in the West Cuts. He figures Bill McCord has been over working in there. Naturally, he was hoping for a chance to get McCord alone."

"And I'm supposed to be able to go over and pick him up in the West Cuts," Kentucky raved.

"Well, he didn't ask no one to pick him up."

"Next thing we'll be tying him on a pack mule," Kentucky growled, and went out like a long-horn bull on the prod.

Going through the kitchen Kentucky Jones caught up his sheep-lined coat with one hand, and a handful of cold French fried potatoes in the other, for he was wolf-hungry yet, and didn't know when he would get a chance to eat again. Out at the corral he picked out a blocky zebra dun horse, dropped his rope on it, and swung his saddle aboard. Two minutes later he was riding westward at a light trot.

In that country of canyon-slashed rimrock no part of

Wolf Bench could be called unbroken; but to the stranger the branching and forking canyons of the West Cuts presented a discouraging maze. The abrupt walls of the canyons, dropping sheer hundreds of feet from the levels of the bench, offered a series of appalling barriers, repeatedly demanding detours of unknown length. Riders long in the rimrock learned a thousand ways to get into those canyons and out of them again; but to the rider who did not know them it too often appeared that there were no ways at all.

Kentucky Jones was anything but familiar with the intricacies of the West Cuts. But he knew the general lay of the land and the typical tricks of canyons; and he knew what men were likely to do who were working stock. He estimated that he had one chance in ten of coming upon either Lee Bishop or the men Lee Bishop sought.

This one chance in ten was, as Kentucky saw it, Lee Bishop's chance for life. He did not believe that Lee Bishop could out-gun Bill McCord, nor that McCord's men would award Bishop an even break. Unhurriedly, Kentucky Jones set out to find Bishop if he could.

For three hours he followed Bishop's trail, sometimes through horse paths that were so dense an overlay of tracks that he could not tell what he had, again for distances where the trail of Lee Bishop's horse lay plain and clear. Then at last a smother of cow tracks blotted out Lee Bishop's trail for a quarter of a mile, and Jones never found where Bishop's trail branched off. He cast ahead, trusting to the general lay of the country to bring him across Bishop's trail again; but though he crossed many a horse track, he accepted none of them as the trail of the horse he sought.

All afternoon he worked through the long loneliness, covering many a weary mile. Twenty riders besides himself might be working the West Cuts for all Kentucky knew; the West Cuts could have hidden a thousand more. Their illimitable emptinesses made a man on a horse seem to crawl like an ant, descending deep hour-long declivities, only to climb again eternally.

He was a long way from home by the time that he decided he must have overshot. Once he had seen two riders, whom he recognized as 88 men, working 88 stock; but Bill McCord was neither one of them. Lee Bishop continued to elude him, lost in the maze. The sun was setting; above Wolf Bench the wrinkled peaks of the Maricopas seemed to float detached from the earth, vast delicate traceries of pale blue shadow, set off with crooked red-gold tracings where the westering sun poured golden light upon the snow. Across Wolf Bench, already in the shadow, a dark bitter-cold breeze began to blow, smelling of frost and blown snow. Kentucky Jones sat his horse upon a high point, and wondered if Lee Bishop were dead.

The frozen wind, forecasting the night, always brought to his mind the things to which a range rider has a right to look forward at that hour: the gleam of a little golden light at a cook-house window, far across the snowy reaches, winking and almost lost in the twilight purple; and the things that the light, seen far off, meant to the rider coming in on his tired horse—the warmth of stove heat, friendly yellow lamp light, the crowding in of red-faced hungry riders, very merry over being done with work, the smell of frying meat and hot fresh bread, and the steam of coffee; and afterward an hour or two of drowsy loafing in the warmth, wise-cracking the day's work, spinning lies—maybe a game of seven-up, and somebody making music for a little while with banjo, mouth organ, or jew's harp.

And at the Bar Hook the cold long twilight, which always made the simple realities of food and snug warmth seem so good, and so well worth living—at the Bar Hook these things should also have meant seeing Jean Ragland again, this girl who, even in adversity, was like no other girl. As Kentucky Jones sat his horse, letting it blow a little from a long climb before putting it upon the long round-about trail home, he was thinking that this range could have been a great range for cattle, and a great range for men, and that maybe having ridden it he never would have wanted to ride another, had things broken as they should. It was a hidden malignance, working under-handedly in the dark, that spoiled this range.

He put the zebra dun into a canyon and out again, and to the rim of another; and there, long after he had let all hope slide, he sighted Lee Bishop at last.

What he saw at first was only a far-off dot creeping across an up-canyon snow-flat; but presently his stock-trained eyes recognized the foreman's horse. He put his pony down into the canyon, then upward through the canyon's notch; and a furlong into the widening valley hailed Lee Bishop across the snow.

"Lee," he demanded as they came together, "what's all

this? You gone crazy, man?"

"I dunno, Kentucky," said Lee Bishop wearily. "Sometimes I think I am. I'm plumb mystified, that's sure."

"You damn fool, you think you can—" A queer look in the other's face stopped him. "What's the matter, Lee? What happened?"

"Well, nothing much; only it's doggone funny!"

"What's funny?"

Lee Bishop pulled up his horse and turned in the saddle to look back. "You see this canyon, Kentucky? I've known this canyon for years. It's called Trap Canyon, because you can't get out the upper end. Over there—and there—and there—" he pointed—"you can get out all right. But the upper end you can't get out. I saw two riders come in here. I'm pretty sure one of 'em was Bill McCord, though I couldn't swear. I followed 'em in. And, by God, Kentucky—they disappeared into thin air!"

"Maybe," offered Kentucky, "they dropped into one of these little coulees. That way they could have worked up to the upper end, where that little drift of timber is."

"Kentucky, I've been to the upper end, and they're not up there, nor any place between. And if they'd gone up them side trails I'd have seen them. You can see a rider two miles as he goes up them long slants."

"Seems kind of peculiar," said Kentucky.

"You're damn tootin' it's peculiar," said Lee Bishop. "I'm plumb confused. And likewise I'm disgusted, and likewise I'm sore. Let's get home." He kicked his horse ahead.

"Wait a minute!" said Kentucky. He held his voice

low. "In God's name, Lee—stop your horse."

"What's the matter?"

"Do what I say," said Kentucky without raising his voice, "and don't ask why. Turn your horse and come back to me." Kentucky Jones turned his own horse so that it was headed back the way Lee Bishop had come. "Now bring your horse alongside of mine, easy," he said. "Walk your horse slow alongside of me."

"Where the devil we going?" Lee Bishop demanded.

"You see that coulee up ahead of us there, about fifty yards? Lee, how deep is that coulee?"

The drainage feature which Kentucky indicated was a shallow twisting cut that wound its way across the floor of the mile-wide canyon, a creek during the rains, a dry wash in time of drought.

"Maybe five or six foot deep," said Bishop. "Why?"

"Walk with me slow and easy until we get to the edge of that coulee," Kentucky said. "Then slap hooks to your horse and jump him into it. Soon as he's in, duck out of the saddle and get down."

Lee Bishop half drew up his horse as if he would stop. "What's got into you, Kentucky?"

"Come on, you fool!"

"See something?"

"I'm not dead sure I did. But, Lee, I'm not going to bet your life I didn't see."

Lee Bishop brought his horse along reluctantly. "Then what the devil was it?" he demanded irritably.

"Don't look back," said Kentucky. "But where the canyon narrows down—right down there where I just rode in, and on the left hand side, it's kind of shelving, and not so very steep; and there's a few junipers there. And I'm not right sure, Lee, but what I saw a tied horse up there; and if it is a horse, he's got his head snaked low to the ground, such as will stop the average horse from whinnying when another one comes along."

Lee Bishop swung in his saddle to stare back at the canyon wall three hundred yards away. Kentucky snarled at him, "Don't turn, you—"

Suddenly Bishop gave a queer gagging cry and snatched at his saddle scabbard. A rifle had spoken from the upper rocks. The gun above spoke a second time, and a third; Bishop's horse started abruptly. The rider, his gun clutched across his breast with both hands, toppled sidewise and pitched headlong into the snow.

Kentucky Jones dropped out of the saddle, one hand taking his bridle reins close to the bit. His pony reared away from the fallen figure; but in another instant Kentucky had the animal under control. He lifted Lee Bishop, and got the foreman over his shoulders. Running diagonally to keep the pony between himself and the ambushed rifle, he tried for the lip of the coulee.

A fourth time the rifle in the rocks spoke, and this time Kentucky's horse plunged, jerking free the reins, and went to its knees. Bishop's rifle fell to the snow and Kentucky turned back two paces to snatch it up. The edge of the coulee was ten paces beyond. As he ran, chest to the ground, the rifle chopped at them once more from the ledges of the notch, and Kentucky felt Lee Bishop's body jerk. Then he lowered Bishop over the edge by the arms, and leaped in after him.

"Lee! Lee, where are you hit?"

Lee Bishop's eyes were squinted shut, and he groaned through set teeth as Kentucky tried to straighten him out upon the bottom of the arroyo. "They got me, Kentucky," he managed to get out at last.

"The hell they have! You going to please that bunch by making a die?"

But when he had examined Lee Bishop he did not know. The first shot Lee Bishop had received had been an angling one, in the back; he could not tell whether the bullet had lodged at the bottom of the lung or some place else.

Catching up Bishop's rifle, Kentucky threw a shot into the general vicinity of the ambush, and instantly drew fire in return. Apparently their attackers were not attempting to close.

Kentucky immediately set about the improvisation of bandages. Twice a minute he interrupted his work to sight across the valley floor for sign of approach. Occasionally also he set his ear to the frozen ground in the bottom of the coulee, but could detect no sound of advance in the cover of the cut.

Still keeping constant lookout, he prepared for the night. Lee Bishop's horse had gone to grazing a quarter of a mile away; he believed he could catch the animal under cover of the dark, but this would do him little good.

Bishop appeared to be too seriously hurt to be moved without aid.

Already the light was uncertain; the molten gold of the last sun still touched the upper peaks of the Maricopas, but the wide reaches of Trap Canyon were pooled in blue dark. Dragging Bishop's rifle with him, Kentucky Jones went out to his dead horse and got his saddle blanket, and the saddle itself to prop Lee's head. He shucked off his sheepskin coat and used it with the blanket to make Bishop a bed in a snow-drifted angle.

Working along the lip of the coulee he collected grease-wood and broken drift, and with this built a tiny fire to warm the wounded man's feet, and another fire at Bishop's side.

Lee Bishop opened his eyes long enough to say faintly, "That'll only be a mark for gunfire, Kentuck."

"I'll take care of that, Lee. It's near dark enough to fire at the flash of the guns."

When these things were done there was nothing more to do but wait, keep watch, and maintain their store of fuel. An hour after dark, walking far up the coulee after more wood, he found a tangled jam of broken branches and bits of rotten log stranded in a backwater; and with this he built a third fire—a signal fire on the edge of the coulee, a hundred yards from their forlorn bivouac. When Campo Ragland and Harry Wilson returned to the Bar Hook it was reasonable to suppose that they would make some effort to find Bishop, who had gone out looking for trouble with every probability of finding it. If they came to look, the signal fire would be visible a long way off. If they did not come to look, Kentucky Jones had a long wait ahead, a wait perhaps equal to the remainder of Lee Bishop's life.

# CHAPTER FIFTEEN

Slowly the hours passed, cold with a bone-piercing cold, and marked only by the imperceptible turn of the stars. After an hour or two Lee Bishop began to mumble from the depths of a delirious stupor; but it must have been nearly midnight when the wounded man's mind cleared.

"Kentucky," he said.

"Right here, Lee."

"I don't know but what I've got my comeuppance, Kentuck."

"That's the bunk, Lee," said Kentucky sharply.

"Don't make me waste my darn breath," said Bishop with a weak irritability. "I got something I got to tell you, Kentuck."

"You better wait until—"

"Shut up! I ought to have told somebody this before; I don't know as it'll do you much good, telling you now. But you ought to know it." Bishop's voice was very faint, but he seemed to speak with little effort, as long as he did not try to raise his tone.

"Lee," said Kentucky, "I don't want to encourage you to talk, but if you can tell me why Bill McCord wants to kill you, it sure might help in what's going to come after this."

"Kentucky, I ain't got any more idea than you," Lee said. "I don't know as I care a whole darn. What I'm worrying about is the way you're getting dragged into this killing of Mason."

"Don't you worry about me. I'm not dragged into it."

"The hell, you're not! Kentuck, what time did you

168

leave the Bar Hook the day Mason was killed?"

"I can prove I was in Waterman by half past one."

"Then," said Bishop, "you couldn't possibly have killed John Mason."

"I never claimed I did, Lee."

"There's others will claim you did," Bishop mumbled. He seemed to trail off, but recovered himself, and his eyes opened wide and clear. "You couldn't have killed Mason," he repeated, "because Mason was still alive when you got back to Waterman. I know he was alive because I saw him alive."

"What time was this?" Kentucky demanded, hitching forward.

"It was between three and four in the afternoon. He was sitting his horse just below a knob, about a quarter mile from the Bar Hook ranch house. Right in there the snow let up for a little bit, and I saw him plain."

"But when you found him," Kentucky pointed out, "there was no snow under him; proving he was killed before the snow began to fall."

"I can't account for that. Maybe the snow under him melted, or something." This seemed unlikely to Kentucky, but he did not interrupt.

"I was a couple furlongs away," Bishop admitted, continuing. "But don't you tell me I made a mistake. I mind how John Mason used to sit, kind of half crooked in the saddle; and I mind the round of his shoulders as he sat his horse, and the tilt of his hat. I'd know him any distance, out of a thousand men."

There was something peculiarly familiar about Lee Bishop's claim of recognition. Suddenly Kentucky knew why. He had heard Joe St. Marie use almost the same words in explaining to Jean Ragland, the night they found Zack Sanders, that he had seen a ghost.

"It isn't hardly likely," Kentucky offered speculatively, "that you'd mistake that pinto horse Mason rode that day."

"They was wrong about that," Bishop said promptly. "That was just one more of them wrong things that came out at the inquest. Mason wasn't riding no pinto horse. He was riding a little blood bay pony—an 88 pony they call Three Spot. . . . I was the other side of Shadow Canyon and I hadn't finished my work; I had a long round-about way to go yet, and was delayed beside, so it was near dark before I got back to the Bar Hook. Though it was not far off from the Bar Hook that I seen him sit."

"Tell me one more thing," Kentucky said. "Did this— did Mason see you?"

"He ought to have seen me. I was in plain sight. But he didn't answer to my wave."

Kentucky rose and went about his work of keeping up the fires. By the signal fire he stood listening for a long time, suspicious of small sounds far away; but he could make certain of no indication of nearby human life. He went back to Lee Bishop.

"Are you there, Kentucky?"

"Right here, Lee."

"Kentucky, I'm sorry I never told that. If only I'd told some people about it, it would clear you. But—use it any way you can."

"You never told anybody at all?"

"Just one person in the world, Kentucky; and that isn't liable to do you much good."

"Who was that?"

"Jean Ragland. . . . She'll back up your word if you tell 'em what I said. But I don't know as it will carry much weight. Anybody can see that she's dead gone on you, Kentuck. Most likely they'll discount what she says in your favor, on that account."

Kentucky Jones said gently, "You're wrong there, Lee."

"You're a fool if you think I am. I told her about seeing Mason, and she made me promise not to tell anybody else. I disremember what I thought was her reason for that; it seemed a reasonable thing to ask, at the time."

Kentucky Jones sucked in his breath through his teeth. "Lee," he said slowly, "you sure you got this straight?"

"Sure, Kentucky. I wouldn't disrecognize Old Iron—"

"I don't mean that, Lee. I mean—you told Jean about seeing this, and she told you not to tell anyone?"

"You beat me, Kentucky. How the hell would a man get a thing like that mixed up?"

"All right, Lee."

"What's the matter with you, Kentuck?"

"There's a link or two missing yet, Lee," Kentucky said. "But I'm dead sure in my own mind, now."

"What are you talking about?"

"You've got me the killer of Mason," Kentucky said.

Lee Bishop started, winced, and settled back again, more limp and more still than before. "You mean," he said at last, "you know who killed Mason?"

"Don't you?"

"I— Listen!"

They were silent for a long moment while Lee Bishop lay with closed eyes, as if the life had gone out of him once and for all.

"There's a horse coming," Bishop said at last.

Kentucky listened, but could hear nothing; it seemed to him that the small purr and hiss of the fire over which he crouched was preventing him from distinguishing far off, fainter sounds. He got up and walked down the gully, past the signal fire, to a place from which he could sight across the flat snow to the canyon narrows. Here the firelight was no longer in his eyes, and the small whisper of the embers could not confuse his ears; and presently he was certain that he distinguished the slow trample of a walking horse. He listened for what seemed a long time, while the sound came sometimes distinct and unmistakable, and again died away until he was half convinced that the rider had turned and drawn off.

Then the sound of the walking hoofs suddenly became sharp and close at hand. Three hundred yards away Kentucky made out the movement of a shadow in shadows, and knew that the rider was sitting his horse in the mouth of the notch. Kentucky Jones freed his rifle's safety catch, carefully, without any click of metal.

For nearly five minutes the rider in the notch sat motionless, and Jones knew that their visitor was watching the signal fire, trying to make out figures near it, or other sign of what the builders of the fire intended.

The rider moved out of the mouth of the notch at last, turned uncertainly to the right, and began to skirt the foot of the canyon wall so slowly that for a little while

Kentucky Jones was inclined to think that there was no rider there at all, but only an unridden horse wandering about in search of its bunch. Moving slowly it circled the signal fire, as if trying to pass at the greatest possible distance. Then the pony passed before a drift of gullied snow which stood like a panel of white set into the grey rock; and against this Kentucky Jones saw the unmistakable silhouette of the figure in the saddle.

The rider turned now, cutting back to circle the signal fire more closely; and at last, as if suddenly impatient, turned directly toward the fire itself and rode to the edge of its circle of light. At a distance of no more than fifty feet, Kentucky Jones slid his rifle over the lip of the coulee and brought it to bear upon the mounted figure.

Then the rider turned; and the firelight showed him Jean Ragland's face.

"Hello, Jean," he said.

Her horse jerked as if it would shy, but its rider sat steady, leaning down to peer into the shadows.

Jean called out sharply, "Is that you, Kentucky? Are you hurt?"

"They hit Lee Bishop, Jean."

She slid out of the saddle, tossing the reins over her pony's head, and came to the edge of the coulee. "Where's Lee?"

"Drop down and I'll take you to him." He held up his arms and she let herself drop into them, but freed herself immediately.

"Is he hit bad?"

He whispered, "He can hear us from here, I think. I don't know but what they've finished him, Jean. He's shot in the side of the back, and Lord knows where the bullet stopped. You shouldn't have come here—don't you know that?"

"Somebody had to come. Campo—my father is back from Waterman; but Harry Wilson quit when Campo wouldn't bring out more riders. You and Campo and I are all that's left. And now poor Lee—poor Lee—"

He led her down the cut to where Bishop lay. The range boss opened his eyes. "Is that you, Jean?"

She dropped on her knees beside him. "Yes, Lee."

"Didn't know but what I might be hearing things. Where's Campo?"

"He's making a sweep of the upper Bench trail. Lee, you must be plumb frozen."

"Pretty near," Bishop admitted.

Jean slipped off her coat, and carefully wrapped Bishop's legs. Then she scrambled out of the cut, ran to her horse and, loosening the cinch, jerked her blanket from under the saddle. When this was placed to suit her, she made ready to go.

"It's sure a shot-to-pieces outfit you bought into, Kentucky."

"That deal is off," he told her. "I own no share in the Bar Hook, nor any part of a share."

Jean looked at him but there was no expression in her face, nor in her voice as she answered. "So you're quitting, too."

"No, not quite yet," Kentucky told her grimly. "I'm just going ahead in a little different way than we figured I was going to; that's all."

Jean dropped beside Lee Bishop again, and for a long

time studied the mask of his face, yellow in the firelight. He seemed asleep. Irrepressible tears appeared on Jean's cheeks, glinting in the light of the fire. She bent over Lee Bishop and kissed him. "Good-by, Lee," she said softly. "I'll be back pretty quick."

Lee Bishop smiled faintly. "Take your time, kid."

Jean caught Kentucky's wrist and led him a little way down the cut. "Do you think there's any chance of moving him?"

"I don't know as we better try, Jean. When you get back to the house, phone to Waterman for Doc Hopper. Then pack a horse and come back. Get hold of a tent if there's any on the place, and all the bed-rolls that come handy, and grub, and bandages, and stuff. You know what we'll need."

Jean Ragland scaled the side of the cut, re-cinched her saddle, and rode off at a sharp trot.

Lee Bishop said, "There goes a great girl, Kentucky. You're lucky, all right."

"Lucky? Me?"

"She'd ride her horse square off the rim," Lee Bishop said, "if you told her to." He was talking in a queer and somehow childish tone of voice which Kentucky had never heard him use. "Listen, Kentucky. Get this—can you hear me all right?"

"I can hear you, Lee."

"You're worse off than you think, Kentucky. Campo believes you killed Mason."

Kentucky said slowly, "I don't know but what Campo has almighty good reason to know better than that, Lee."

"What if he has?" Lee demanded. "What you don't

know is, he's been gathering up stuff against you—tracing guns, and the like of that. In a pinch he'll turn on you, Campo will! But believe in that girl. She believes in you; and she'll stand by you."

"The pinch will come quick, now," Kentucky said. "But she'll not be with me, Lee."

Lee Bishop said in a curious hoarse whisper, "She'd jerk the heart out of her, if you needed it. She's got a faith in you that you don't have for her."

"Faith?" Kentucky repeated savagely. "If she'd trusted me only half way, only quarter way, you and I wouldn't be sitting here tonight."

Lee Bishop looked at Kentucky a long time, and his mind seemed to be turning vague. "You ain't licked, Kentucky," he said at last, weakly. "You can beat this game yet."

"Sure I'll beat it," Kentucky assured him. "Lee, I'll beat it in spite of her!"

Lee Bishop said in a queer voice, "You—you couldn't go against that girl, Kentucky."

"I'd sooner cut off my right hand, Lee; but I've got to go square against her now."

For another long moment Lee Bishop fixed staring, vacant eyes upon Kentucky's face. "You love her, huh?" he said.

Kentucky Jones shivered; he felt as if the grip of the night cold was getting the better of him, so that his body had a core of ice. He covered his face with his hands. "I think," he said, "I hate her as I've never hated any living thing in my life."

Lee Bishop's words jerked out of him incoherently,

but unexpectedly sharp and strong. "God help you, Kentucky—don't say that!"

"All right, Lee."

Jean Ragland made the round trip—and loaded a mule at the other end—in a little over four hours, which was wonderful time on those night trails. But she might as well have saved her animals; for an hour before she reached Trap Canyon again Lee Bishop was dead.

## CHAPTER SIXTEEN

When Kentucky had packed the body of Lee Bishop to the Bake Pan camp of the Bar Hook, where he placed it with that of Jim Humphreys, he faced his horse into the steep switchback trail up the rim, and started for the main ranch; the mule, freed of half its burden, followed the horse, unled.

Kentucky had agreed with Jean Ragland that to take Lee Bishop to the Bake Pan camp was a shorter and more convenient pack; and Kentucky had seized upon the opportunity to release Jean from the mournful procession and send her home.

He now put his horse up the trail stiffly, climbing fast. He felt no weariness, but only a black temper. Now that he knew for the first time what set of ugly circumstances he was up against, he knew what he had to do; it was not easy, and he wanted to get it behind him.

On the edge of the rim he paused, while his eyes swept all the visible Bench. The voices of the guns and the circumstances of Lee Bishop's death had brought him an odd new alertness, an almost painful consciousness of everything that moved within the limits of the rimrock horizon. It was as if he had found himself returned to the days of his forefathers, when an awareness of far-off details had a lot to do with keeping on a man's scalp. Long before Jean Ragland came in sight, he knew that two horses were coming toward him along the trail, that they had but one rider, and that the second horse was not driven, but led.

For a moment after Jean came in sight he was absorbed by the sight of her. She rode a little dark pony, and her short white storm coat was in key with the snow. Hardly anybody ever saw Jean Ragland ride without following her with his eyes, as a man looks after a bird that is a bright living decoration against the snow. And now the girl and the pony she rode looked better because the led horse was raw-boned and mud colored, with only a sharp, well-tracked leg action to suggest that it might be more horse than at first it seemed.

As they met in the trail he saw that her face was quiet with the resignation which had characterized it for the last two days; but her eyes were alive. They looked very dark and tragically comprehending, as if she were able to see behind men and events to fatalities which she opposed without any chance of victory. But there was also in her eyes a touch of feverish light which told him that she was still fighting, though what she was fighting, or how, he was no longer sure that he knew.

"I've brought you a fresh horse," she said immediately. "Maybe it doesn't look like much horse, but it is a whole lot of horse. Pretty near any Bar Hook horse would give down under you before this plug would."

"I suppose I kind of ought to appreciate that," Kentucky said; "but, Jean, how come you think I am going to need such a long-traveling horse?"

"Kentucky," she said, "Kentucky—" She drew her hand across her eyes, as if what she was trying to say was almost beyond her ability. "Look here. I've asked a lot of favors of you, Kentuck; a lot more than I ever had any right to ask. But it seems like you never questioned that part of it."

"I don't remember when this was," he said; "but go ahead."

Her mouth and eyes were taut. "I have to ask you one thing more. If you'll do this one thing more for me, I'll be grateful to you all my life; and I swear I'll never ask anything of you again."

"Jean, girl," Kentucky said, "what's happened here?"

"Take this horse, and the mule, and such of the stuff as you need. I don't need to tell you where to go or how to get there, nor how to get along; but do as I say! Go a long way, and go fast, and lose yourself; and never come back until some day this thing is over with and forgotten!"

Kentucky Jones stared at her a long time, studying her face; but her eyes did not flinch from his. At last a crooked one-sided smile changed his mouth.

"I know that this is a terrible sacrifice for you," Jean said. Desperation came into her voice, bred of the hopelessness of making him see the necessity she urged. "I wouldn't ask you this, Kentucky, I swear I wouldn't, if I wasn't positive that there's no other way. Believe this— I'll be your friend, always; it may be later that I can help you, and send your money to you, or something like that.

179

That will work out later. All I can say now is that I'd rather be dead than sitting here telling you this, but there isn't any other way."

"Why do you ask this?" Kentucky said curiously.

"Kentucky—God forgive me!—I can't answer that! But I tell you that there isn't any time to lose! Not an hour, not even—I can't tell you any more! I can only—"

"You'll have to tell me, I think," Kentucky said. His face was hard, and the fatigue that she had been unable to detect before now had carved lines about his mouth, emphasizing the crooked line of his broken nose.

"You've got to do what I say," she told him passionately, "without any question of why about it."

"You hardly expected me to do that, I think," he told her.

Jean cried out sharply, "Don't! Take the horse and go. Kentucky, as you love me—but you don't love me; I know that."

"I think," he said, "just now it doesn't matter a whole lot who loves who, or who doesn't."

There was a touch of hysteria in her voice as she answered him. "No, not to you—I think you don't care anything about anybody in the world!"

"God help the man who does," he said. "As for taking that horse and making a run of it, I'm sorry not to do something that you ask. But I can't imagine anything on the face of the earth that would make me do that now."

"Then," she said quickly, "I'll tell you why you must. My father—my father—" It seemed for a moment as if she were unable to go on. But she pulled herself together and spoke evenly, her words distinct and quick. "You know by this time why Bob Elliot is swamping the Bar Hook range. You have eyes that see things—I don't think anyone can hide from you what a thing means. You can't make me think that you don't know why Elliot has no fear of Campo, nor the Bar Hook."

"No," he said slowly, "I wouldn't pretend that I can't see that."

Her words tumbled out of her incoherently. "It's because Bob Elliot was close to the Bar Hook when Mason was killed. Poor Lee Bishop knew that—though I don't think he knew that he knew it. I—"

Kentucky Jones said, "Bishop told me that he knew."

"And now," said Jean, "now I've got to tell you that I've known this all along—almost from the first. And I—"

"You're sure you want to tell me this, Jean?"

"I have to tell you—you make me tell you—"

That was a strange meeting, there on the trail in all that dazzle of sun-whipped snow, while all the sharp, sad, hidden things that this girl had never meant to tell a living soul came trembling out of her in a panicky disorder. Perhaps he should have wept or gathered her in his arms; but he could not.

"All right," he said. "What, exactly, is Bob Elliot holding over your father?"

"Somehow he's guessed the truth: that—whoever killed Mason killed him with my father's rifle. I knew that when I put the bullet into your hand at the inquest; I've known for days that you must know that too, though you said nothing to me."

"Yes," he admitted, "I figured out that."

"And Bob Elliot knows it—I'm certain he knows it. Though I swear I don't know how he is so sure."

"But you yourself are sure that it is true—that the murderer used your father's rifle?"

"The—the—yes; I'm virtually certain of that. And my father knows it. He—"

"Have you talked this over with him?"

"No—how could I? It's changed him so I hardly know him. He used to have a terrible fighting temper—but where is it now? He doesn't dare come to a showdown with Elliot; he's afraid of the effect the shock would have on my mother."

"And on you."

"On my mother," she repeated. "He doesn't dare face it out because of her. But just as he won't fight Elliot because of that—something in his makeup keeps him from protecting himself, too. Nothing would bring him to hide evidence—though that evidence might turn against him, as well as against the true murderer. He must have known—"

"Then," said Kentucky, "his alibi—about being somewhere else at the time Mason was killed—is not so good as some people have been led to suppose?"

"He hasn't any testimony in support of it but mine. They'll discount that, because I'm his daughter; even— even if they don't break my testimony in some other way."

He did not stop to tell her that he knew by this that her support of Campo's alibi had been perjury. Instead he asked her, "How many people know that Campo—your father set out to kill Bob Elliot the day Mason was killed?"

She cried out with a shudder in her voice, "You even know that?"

"Bob Elliot told me that," he said shortly.

Jean Ragland looked dizzy, and sick. "Then who can tell how many people Bob Elliot has told?"

Kentucky Jones stripped off his gloves and made himself a cigarette. "And how many people," he said slowly, "do you think can tell a living man from a ghost?"

Her voice quavered irregularly, no longer fully under her control. "What do you mean?"

"There used to be a picture hanging in the Bar Hook ranch house," Kentucky said. "A picture in a dark wood frame that had acorns at the corners. That picture was stolen because somebody thought it had something to do with the Mason case. When you saw that that picture was stolen, you were panic-stricken, and hid the empty frame from your father. Now I'm going to tell you what that picture was."

"You can't—you never saw—"

"It was a picture of a man on a horse. When you first looked at that picture it seemed to be an enlarged snapshot of Bob Elliot. Only—when you looked close, it was not Elliot, but John Mason. Do you deny that, Jean?"

"No," said Jean miserably. "You see? It's just as I said. Nothing escapes you, nothing's able to hide itself away from you. That—that's the rest of the case against my father. Lee Bishop didn't know who it was he saw near the Bar Hook when he thought he saw Mason, and Joe St. Marie only thought he saw Mason's ghost. But—

when they rested sideways in their saddles with their faces hidden, a long way off in the dark anybody could mistake Bob Elliot for Mason."

"Or," he said, "an angry man might—just possibly— *mistake Mason for Elliot.*"

She drew a deep breath and pressed her gloved fingers against her eyes, but did not reply.

"It's my belief," Kentucky said, "that it was the sheriff who searched the house—or had it searched; in which case, he must have that picture."

"I think you're right about the sheriff; he must have been looking for the gun to match the Mason bullet. But he didn't take the picture of Mason—because I took it myself."

"*You* did? But you looked so scared—"

"I didn't hide frame and all, at first, because it left a pale spot on the wall, that Dad would have noticed. I meant to slide some other picture into the frame. But I forgot it. And then, with Dad hunting all through the house, to see what had been taken, I thought he'd notice the empty frame—and I was terrified."

"And that rifle—" He paused, watching her, and licked shut his cigarette.

"The rifle!" she burst out, jerking her hand away from her eyes. "Who knows where that is now? How do we know that Bob Elliot doesn't have it himself? Sheriff Hopper has the other bullet. If ever the bullet is fitted to my father's gun—"

"No," he said, "Bob Elliot doesn't have the rifle."

Her voice rose hysterically. "How do you know he hasn't?"

"Because," he told her, "that rifle is dismounted and hidden in the mattress of your bed."

She stared at him blankly for a long moment. "Oh, dear Lord," she said at last in a broken voice. "Why did I ever try to hide anything from you?" She did not avert her face from him, but she turned her eyes to the Maricopas, sitting very straight in the saddle. "Yes, I hid it. Campo must have known at once that Mason was killed with his rifle; but do you think anything in the world could have persuaded him to do away with that rifle, to pitch it into the bottom of some canyon?"

Watching her face in half profile he saw her begin to cry, silently, and without tears. "Is that all?" he said.

"That's one side of it." She steadied herself.

"And what's the other side?"

"The other side is that he—he thinks that—that you might have killed Mason, Kentucky."

He said slowly, "Jean, are you lying to me again?"

She rushed ahead, a little of her color returning. "With everything against my father, what could I do but keep silent?"

"And hide what evidence you could," said Kentucky.

She looked at him squarely as she repeated after him, "And hide what evidence I could."

"And now you want me to jump the country."

"For your own sake," she said quickly. "I swear to God, Kentuck, it's for your own sake I want you to do that. All the time he's spent in Waterman, when we didn't know what he was doing, he's been trying to build a case against you. Everybody knows you were at the house at about the time Mason was killed. The house was open, and anyone could have got to the guns. Campo's figured all along that only one thing was lacking to—to implicate you so deeply in the death of Mason that you could never—"

"And that one thing lacking was my reason for killing Mason."

"Yes, of course—and now he thinks he has it. Maybe he would have held off still, but Lee Bishop's killing has driven him wild. He's phoned Waterman. Sheriff Hopper is coming out. I don't know what he has or how he dug it up and put it together—but this I know: that he believes that he can show that you had a motive for killing John Mason stronger than anyone else could possibly have had. I—"

"Jean, do you think he believes I killed Mason?"

This time she averted her face; when she spoke her voice was hardly audible. "I only know that he would be glad to believe it—if he could."

"If he could," repeated Kentucky. He turned his horse toward the Bar Hook with a savage twist of the bit.

Jean cried out, "Where are you going?"

"I'm going to hang me the man that killed Old Ironsides."

"Kentucky, wait!" She booted her horse against his and caught his arm in both hands. "Kentucky, if it weren't for me you'd never have been in this. This isn't your fight—it's never been your fight. It's mine and my father's. You're not tied into it as we are. You—"

"I'm tied into it now."

"No, no! Take your horse and ride out. Take—"

"I'll go," he told her, "when I've done this job of work."

She stared at him, her mouth twisted and quivering. "Kentucky, if there's anything in the world that I can do or say—"

He said, "I'm going to clear this thing if it splits the rimrock wide open."

"Then—then, Kentucky, can't we work it out together? If anybody in the world can make my father see reason, I can. I'll help you in every way I can, if only—"

"Ask yourself," he said, "if you've ever helped me yet? Ask yourself if you've ever told me anything, or allowed me to find out anything for myself if you could prevent it? Not two minutes ago you lied to me about the rifle!"

She said, "Just the same, you're the only one I've looked to for—"

His face was like the grey rock. "I'm just what you said I was a few minutes ago: an outsider here—an outsider to your father, and an outsider to you. I don't blame you for protecting your father. But I can tell you that if you had trusted me even so far as—"

Her head went up, and her face was white as doeskin. "Why should I trust you?"

"Why should you?" he repeated. He yanked his horse into the trail; and this time she did not stop him.

## CHAPTER SEVENTEEN

Kentucky Jones came into the Bar Hook layout on the dead run, dropped off his horse at the door and went pushing into the house. He made his way straight to the little crank-sided wall telephone, and belled Waterman.

It was one of the deputies who, after a prolonged delay, finally answered from Sheriff Hopper's office.

"Talking from the Bar Hook," Kentucky said. "Has Sheriff Hopper left yet?"

"Yeah, he left about three minutes ago," came the voice from Waterman, indistinct behind a fluttering and crackling in the line. "Wait, now! Yeah, there goes his car by, in the street."

"Run out and catch him," Kentucky yelled into the phone. "Shout your lungs out—but stop him!"

Over the line came the rattle of a dropped receiver. Kentucky Jones could make out the slam of a door, and a vague shouting sound that died after a moment behind the sputter of the line.

There followed a protracted wait. It seemed to Kentucky Jones that an hour passed while he stood at the telephone waiting for the deputy to return. This was the sort of small chance, he was thinking, which made or broke the run of the cards. A difference of three minutes in time was promising to rob him of all opportunity. But the wire opened again at last, and it was not the deputy who came back to the phone.

"This is Floyd Hopper speaking," said the small voice from Waterman. "Who's that?"

"This is Kentucky Jones at the Bar Hook."

"Oh, yeah? What the hell do you want?"

"I've found out something. Do as I say and you'll have your man in six hours."

"Why the devil should I do like you say?" came Hopper's voice, sourly.

"I'll give you proof," said Kentucky. "If I'm wrong you can tell me to go to hell. All I ask is that you test it for yourself."

"And when is all this going to be?" said the sheriff.

"Right now," said Kentucky. "You can shake down the proof of what I know in less than five minutes from right where you sit."

There was a long pause at the other end of the wire. Kentucky was almost ready to jiggle the hook, to see if the connection had been broken. "What is it you want, Jones?" came Hopper's voice at last.

"Have you got the bullets that killed Zack Sanders?" Kentucky said.

"Of course I've got 'em!"

"And you've got the gun that was found in Sanders' hand."

"Well?"

"Take the bullets that killed Sanders and compare them with the gun that was in Zack Sanders' hand when he was found dead. You'll find that Zack Sanders was killed with the gun that was found in his own hand."

An instant's pause was followed by an oath that scorched the wires. "Jones, you fool with me—by God, I'll learn you to fool with me!"

"All I say is look at 'em! It won't cost you the time it took me to get you on the phone. I'm giving you your chance to get the man that killed Mason. You can do what you want to about it."

"I suppose," came Hopper's voice, "you figure Zack Sanders committed suicide!"

"Take a look," Kentucky repeated. "Fire a bullet from Zack's gun, and match it against those he was killed with. If I'm right call me back, and I'll give you the lay. Otherwise, you can go lamming around here blind until it's too late—it's all one to me." Kentucky Jones smashed the receiver onto the hook.

He turned to find Campo Ragland standing in the doorway.

Kentucky Jones leaned against the wall. He crossed his legs, and rolled a cigarette; and the two looked at each other. Campo seemed almost literally to have increased in stature since Kentucky Jones had seen him last. His long bowed legs set him high up in the world; it was the lean breadth of his shoulders and a stooping carriage which prevented him from appearing to be as big a man as he was. And his big head, made to appear more massive by the broad receding sweep of forehead which his thinning hair had left, helped to detract from his appearance of height. But the indeterminate stoop of Campo's carriage was now gone; and as he stood with his big freckle-blotched hands holding the side of the doorway he made the doorway look small. Kentucky saw that he was armed.

Campo said slowly, "Think you can head it off, do you?"

"Maybe I do," Kentucky answered.

"I heard what you said over the phone just now."

Campo's voice was lowered; but he sounded as if he had accused Kentucky of misbranding a calf.

"I knew you were listening. I heard you come in."

"I suppose," said Campo, "you've got more guts than any man on the face of this rocky up-ended earth!"

"Maybe I have," said Kentucky. "Maybe if I didn't have I wouldn't be here now."

"And you'd be better off," Campo told him.

Nobody could have said exactly when Kentucky's face had changed; but anyone looking at him now would have seen that he had small ugly eyes, and that the broken line of his nose was made uglier by the crooked line of his mouth, from one corner of which his cigarette now trailed. He stood relaxed, motionless; he might have been carved there except for the tenuous blue thread of smoke from his cigarette, rising in a wavering, swaying line before his face.

"I've heard tell that the west is dead," he said. "And I always thought that was funny, with the land still here, and the cattle, and the riders working in the saddle like they always worked. But when the owner of a brand sets to working in the dark, and shoves one of his own riders into the noose because he's afraid to face out the music himself—I guess the west is gone, all right."

Campo faced him in silence for a little while, and the blood came up into his head, darkening his wind-reddened face. "Before a man can clean a range," he said, his voice low, "he must first clean his own outfit."

"So you think," said Kentucky, "you can convict me of killing John Mason?"

Campo snapped at him, "Who told you that?"

"I've been taken for a fool here," said Kentucky. "I expect maybe a fool is what I am, for I've let myself be used as a fool. But I'm not a blind man, and you should have allowed for that. So you think you can make it stick, do you?"

Campo Ragland still stood in the doorway as he had before, with his hands against the frame on either side; but Kentucky Jones knew that the man was tight as a banjo string. He did not miss the flick of Campo's eyes as they dropped for an instant to Kentucky's holstered gun.

"What I can make stick and what won't stick," Campo said, "I don't pretend like I know. I only know what I'm convinced of in my own mind."

"As, for instance?"

"As, for instance," repeated Campo, his eyes red and steady on Kentucky's face, "that you like to ruined us all when you shot John Mason down."

They looked at each other for a moment more, then Kentucky Jones moved his hands to the buckle of his belt. He saw the quick start of Campo Ragland's right hand toward his holster; but Kentucky only loosed his belt and tossed it aside.

"You needn't fret yourself," said Kentucky. "You're never going to get a gunfight out of me, Campo."

Campo said, "I expect not. But if you're holding off because you're gone on my girl, you can pick your gun belt up again. Because no damn sneaking killer is fit to so much as walk where her shadow's been."

In the little pause Kentucky heard the outer door of the kitchen open and close, and knew that Jean had come.

"Maybe you're right," he said. "Maybe I couldn't ever bring myself to gun you, because of the reason you've named. Maybe, if it wasn't for just that one thing, you'd have been talking for your life, Campo, these many days ago."

Campo Ragland's voice rose hard and tight. "If you think you can—" He checked himself.

"I don't think about what I could have done, because that's past. But I'm asking myself why you don't sing mighty small."

"What's the meaning of that?" Ragland snarled.

"I'll give you just one little pointer as to what's the meaning of that. Where's the rifle that killed John Mason? You don't know. But I know! And I could lay hands on it now."

The rounded receding sweep of Campo's forehead was marked with tortuous distended veins that stood out in bold relief in the unfavorable slant of the light. "Bring it out then," Campo cried out. "If you think I'm afraid to have that rifle brought out—"

"No," said Kentucky. "It isn't me that you're afraid of. It wasn't that, that sent you prowling around in the dark trying to find a way to deliver up another man. It's the man that's swamping your range, while you sit by and watch your riders go out and get shot."

"If you mean I'm afraid of Bob Elliot," said Campo, "you lie, and I put it to your face. And when it comes to you—come out with what you've got, and all you've got! I'd rather be dead than think you held back from it for the sake of—for the reason you're trying to make me think."

"Put that reason out of your head," said Kentucky. "When this thing's over I'm going to turn my back on the batch of you, and move on."

"No," said Campo, his voice very deep and strong, but shaken with a repressed turbulence, "you'll never be moving on." He came into the room and stood close in front of Kentucky, red-eyed as a roused bear. "Not any more," he said again. "You hear me? I've found out what you supposed nobody would ever find out. I found out that you had more reason to kill Mason than any living man!"

"And I'll make it easy for you," said Kentucky. "I'll admit it."

Ragland stared at him a moment, thunder-struck. "You—you—what?"

Suddenly Kentucky laughed in his face, silently, with an ugly twist of the mouth. "You're a fool, Campo," he said.

Campo Ragland blew up. "I've stood enough," he shouted, his voice rising in a shuddering gust. He snatched up Kentucky's gun belt and tried to thrust it into his hands. "Take your gun belt, and I'll give you the break! Take it and draw!"

"And if I don't?" said Kentucky.

"Then I'll see you crack your neck at the end of a rope!"

There was a small sound behind Campo Ragland, voiced inarticulately, like a word that had tried to make itself heard and could not. Looking past Campo, Kentucky saw that Jean was standing in the doorway where her father had stood.

Her words broke throatily, jerked and twisted, forcing their way out against an all but overmastering emotion. Yet they carried no inflection of appeal, but instead were bitter with an insupportable conviction.

"No! No, no, no! You'll never do that!"

Campo Ragland whirled. "What—what—"

The room in which they stood was shadowy, and the doorway was bright with light, so that they saw her in grey silhouette, with only the red-gold backlight upon her hair to give her figure color; and the shadows half concealed the quiver of her lips, the pallor of her face. But shadow could not hide the tormented intensity of her eyes.

"I'll never what?" her father demanded in a strange taut voice, like the ring of overdrawn wire.

"You—you'll never deliver up Kentucky Jones!"

Campo's voice rose to a thunder. "And why will I not?"

"Because—when you do—I'll tell them all the truth!"

Her father's face went empty as he stared at his daughter, as if faced by an enormity too great for him to comprehend. For a moment he wavered as if his mind refused comprehension, like a horse refusing a jump. "What truth?" he managed to get out at last. "What are you talking—"

Jean's voice, broken, all but hysterical, cut him down. "You—you know—what truth! If I tell what I know, it's you that'll be hooked for the murder of Mason!"

Watching Campo, Kentucky saw the boss of the Bar Hook fold up. His height left him, and all the strength and aggression went out of his wide lean shoulders, and a ragged palsy came into his hands. In those moments Campo Ragland turned, before their eyes, into an old man; and his voice was old, quavering, and weak, and ineffectual, as he tried to speak. "Why, Jean—" he faltered; "why—Jean—Jean—"

His daughter stood rigid, shoulders up, and arms stiff at her sides, her eyes wide with the glazed brilliance of frozen waterholes as she watched her father. Then her breath caught in her throat, and she began to sob brokenly; and her face streamed with the tears that had been held back for so long.

"Child, child," said Kentucky softly, "you didn't need to do that!"

Jean cried out, "Don't talk to me! Don't—"

The telephone ripped the quiet apart with a whirring clamor.

Kentucky stepped to the phone and took the receiver down. "Well?"

"Who's that?" came the small voice over the wire.

"Kentucky Jones, at the Bar Hook."

"This is Floyd Hopper. Kentucky, you sure got me up in the air. There ain't any question about it—Sanders was killed with the gun that was found in his hand!"

"Well?"

"It's your move, Kentucky. By God, it sure is time this thing was cleared up! What goes on here, man? Put a name to it!"

Jean said in a strangled sort of voice, "Is that the sheriff?"

"Just a minute, Hopper," Kentucky said, and turned to Jean.

"What—what are you going to do?"

"What can I do? Your father has stampeded us all. If I'd had another week I could have gentled this thing, but now the whole works has blown up under us. All we can do is try to ride it through to a finish, now!" He turned back to the phone. "Tell you what you do," he said, slow and distinct into the phone. "Are you there, Hopper?"

"Yes, I'm here."

"Go get Ted Baylor. Arrest him if you have to, but get him. Give a deputy the job of keeping hold of him, and don't let him out of your sight until this thing is cleared up!"

"I've already got Ted Baylor," came the sheriff's voice from Waterman. "I had that from Campo before you called. What's the matter with you fellers out there?"

For a moment Kentucky Jones faltered, and his face went blank, but he spoke to the phone again. "All right. Then go out to the 88 and get Bill McCord."

"That's liable to be a job for a regiment," said Hopper.

"Then get your regiment. When you've got both Ted Baylor and Bill McCord, bring them out here."

"What if Bob Elliot wants to come along with Bill McCord?" the sheriff asked. "McCord is Elliot's foreman. Elliot'll probably want to come along and stand by."

"If Elliot wants to come, let him. I don't care what Elliot does. You bring Baylor and McCord. When you've done that, I'll give you the man that killed Mason."

"Which of 'em is it?" the sheriff demanded.

"Hold the rope a minute." Kentucky turned to where

Campo Ragland sat, his hands dangling limply over the arms of his chair; he was staring vaguely at the wall, and his mouth was slightly open, as though he might be a thousand miles deep in thought. "Campo," Kentucky demanded, "why did you send for Ted Baylor?"

Campo Ragland, returning slowly from the distances, stared at Kentucky a moment, almost as if without recognition. Then he got up and walked toward the door, slowly and unsteadily, like an aged man. His voice was hardly more than a whisper. "To hell with you," he said.

Kentucky turned back to the phone. "I said," came Sheriff Hopper's voice, "which one of 'em is it?"

"Neither one," said Kentucky. He hung up the receiver.

## CHAPTER EIGHTEEN

The long dusk of the winter rim had given way to night, star bright and frostily clear, before a car was heard upon the Waterman road. Kentucky Jones walked out alone in shirt sleeves.

"Where's Campo?" Sheriff Hopper demanded, climbing out from behind the wheel.

"He's here. Come on in."

Into the light of the kitchen Sheriff Floyd Hopper now herded the four other men who were with him. They were Ted Baylor, whose eyes were alert and watchful, and perhaps slightly puzzled in a poker face; Bill McCord, grimly expressionless; Bob Elliot, looking sardonic and self-sufficient; and a blonde Norwegian-faced young deputy named Willie Helmar.

"You-all just have a cup of coffee and make yourselves

at home," Kentucky said. "Sheriff, Campo and I would like to talk to you a minute, here in the other room."

"All right," Hopper said.

"You fellers sure are a secretive bunch," Bob Elliot grumbled, warming his hands over the stove.

"Come on in, if you want to, Bob," Kentucky said. "You might just as well sit in on this."

Elliot accepted, following as Kentucky led the way through the main living room to a little room at one side, which the boss of the Bar Hook used as a sort of office. This room was small, and its gunracks and deer horns made it seem smaller, as if there were hardly room for the three men to find places here. Kentucky Jones could not look at this trophy-cluttered room, which gave a curious effect of being a cross section of Campo Ragland's soul, without thinking of that other contrasting room at the other end of the house, which belonged to Jean's mother. So different must have been the people that made those rooms that the wonder was not that Mrs. Ragland was now far away, but that she had ever been able to make herself a part of this household at all.

Here among his things Campo sat, backed into a corner. His heavy desk was pulled diagonally across in front of him, as if he were at bay there, futilely barricaded. He sat on the small of his back, his chin dropped upon his chest; from beneath the sweeping dome of forehead his eyes regarded them as redly as the eyes of a dog in firelight. Suddenly Kentucky wondered if Campo's evident sense of standing stubbornly at bay had been caused more by himself and Sheriff Hopper than by the now far-off woman who had made him fear a showdown upon Mason's death—so fear it that he was held in a paralysis of indecision while Jim Humphreys was killed, and Lee Bishop, and the 88 herds poured over his range.

In the shadows of a recessed window-seat Jean Ragland sat, her feet drawn up under her so that she looked very small and no more conspicuous there than a kitten.

Sheriff Hopper said, "Howdy, Campo; howdy, Miss Ragland."

Campo flicked him a glance, then dropped surly red eyes to his thick freckle-blotched hands; his mouth moved as if he were about to spit, but remained closed.

Kentucky Jones began the making of a cigarette. "Seems like we been a little bit disorganized out here, Hopper," he said. "The fact is Campo and I haven't seen eye to eye on this, in all things."

Sheriff Floyd Hopper waited; and Bob Elliot, who had made himself comfortable in an easy chair, crossed his legs and laced his fingers together.

"It seems," said Kentucky, "that Campo became convinced that I did away with Old Ironsides myself."

There was a sharp silence here during which Kentucky Jones finished and lighted his cigarette. Hopper turned a questioning glance on Campo. "Yes?"

Ragland glanced at Kentucky Jones, but did not speak.

"Everybody's known all along," Kentucky said, "that I was out here at the Bar Hook just before snow flew on the day Mason was killed; and I've admitted it. Assuming for a minute that I could easily have got hold of the weapon that killed Mason, the next thing needed

200

against me was my reason for this act of unseemly violence. Campo found out where I did have a good reason—and naturally figured that he'd come to the end of the trail."

"You admit you had a reason for killing Mason?" Hopper said.

"I'm not denying that I had," said Kentucky. "Come to find out, that was one of the reasons that Campo Ragland wanted Ted Baylor brought out here. Ted is one of the very few that know that Mason turned me down on a renewal that I'd counted on—and like to broke me."

"You're broke, Jones?"

"Close to it."

"You sure are free-handed about making a case against yourself!"

"Campo was overlooking a couple of things," said Kentucky. "It's true that you can show I was broke by Mason. But what about all those other cowmen that Mason had to close down on? To those men Mason's decisions meant salvation or ruin—exactly as to me. He could not carry us all. In digging up a reason for me to kill Mason, Campo only dug up a motive that forty or fifty rimrock cowmen would own to."

"I see what you're driving at," said Hopper. "But you're getting the whole thing scattered out and shuffled again, like cattle turned loose after a roundup. Maybe Mason did have such an enemy, or six of them, or fifty; the fifty of them weren't having no barbecue at the Bar Hook the day Mason was killed."

"So I gathered," Kentucky admitted. "But bear in mind this—if any one of the fifty had been there, he might have gun-whipped Mason. The bad times have borne down mighty heavy on Wolf Bench. For a year and a half here the brands have been on edge, watching each other and suspicious of each other. There's plenty gun smoke in the history of the rim; and in a time like this, that gun smoke comes up out of the past and gets men's minds fogged up. There's been an awful lot of wearing of guns in the rimrock the past ten, twelve months, what with riders hoping for a chance to shoot a coyote, or a rabbit—with a .45 slug! Cowmen's minds can work that way only about so long before something boils over and busts."

"Yes," Hopper admitted, "I was looking for it all right; but when it come to killing Mason—"

"He was a right ambitious victim," Kentucky agreed; "but there were big reasons for killing him, too. When you build up pressure like that you can figure on an explosion. But it was the gun smoke in the history, and the pressure of the bad times, that wiped out John Mason—and incidentally Zack Sanders."

"And Jim Humphreys and Lee Bishop," the sheriff put in.

"That's partly true," Kentucky allowed; "the killing of Humphreys and Bishop sure do make up an angle of this thing. It took two things to kill off Humphreys and Bishop—the smoky feeling between the brands before Mason's death, and Mason's death itself. Humphreys and Bishop were killed in the weirdest damn one-sided range struggle that has ever been seen on this or any other range."

The sheriff said slowly, "Mason's death comes first.

But don't you ever think, Elliot, that I've forgotten the funny look of this so-called range war that's rubbed out Humphreys and Bishop. Everybody knows you've swamped Campo's range; and Campo's hardly raised his hand against it. I'll tell you plain, Elliot, if Bishop and Humphreys were killed in the kind of shenanigan it looks like, I'll—"

Bob Elliot reddened. "I didn't come here to talk about range rights," he said, "but if you want a showdown on that, I'm ready, any time. As long as there's been cattle run on the rim, or on the Bake Pan either, no brand has ever leaned any harder against another brand than the Bar Hook has borne down on the 88. If Campo's pulled in his horns, maybe it's because he knows that the rights of the 88 are going to be backed up for a change."

Campo Ragland spoke for the first time. "Rights!" he said bitterly. "Rights!"

Sheriff Floyd Hopper said angrily, "You're a funny one, Elliot, to bring in talk about rights!"

"You said yourself," Elliot answered, "the Bar Hook has folded up."

They all turned their eyes to Campo Ragland; but the boss of the Bar Hook was rolling a cigarette with slow meticulous care, and he did not contribute any observations.

Sheriff Floyd Hopper swung restively in his seat. "I can't understand it," he said. "I can't understand it."

"You'll understand it now," said Kentucky Jones. "I can tell you exactly why Elliot has thought he could shove his beef all over Bar Hook range in full peace and comfort."

Bob Elliot said, "If the idea is to sit here half the—"

"Let him alone, Bob," Hopper snapped.

Kentucky Jones looked Elliot over with a cool unfriendly eye. "I'll tell you another little thing that happened the day Mason was killed," he said. "Bob Elliot and Campo Ragland were riding the Bake Pan range; and it happened that they met on that ride."

"Where did you get this?" Hopper put in.

"Partly," Kentucky said, "from Elliot himself."

Elliot said, "I'll be damned if—"

"Will you be still?" said Sheriff Hopper. "What then, Jones?"

"Elliot was armed; Campo Ragland was not. It seems to be a kind of custom with the 88 to take advantage of a situation like that—as Lee Bishop and I found out one day in a little conversation we had with Bill McCord. Naturally I wasn't there when Ragland and Elliot met; but I can tell you that what happened was this—Elliot gave Ragland such a cussing out as you couldn't hardly expect any man to stand for, or put up with."

"Is that right, Campo?" the sheriff demanded.

Campo Ragland gave a grunt which might have been an affirmative; it did not appear to be a denial.

"Campo Ragland," said Kentucky Jones, "told Bob Elliot that he would kill him before the day was out."

"He's guessing now," said Bob Elliot.

"Yes, guessing," conceded Kentucky Jones.

Campo Ragland said unexpectedly, "Yes, by God— but he's guessing right!"

Kentucky Jones nodded. "Sure I'm guessing right! Up here in the Frying Pan country there's an old lion hunter called Old Man Coffee; and he says—"

"To hell with Old Man Coffee," said the sheriff. "What happened then?"

"Just at the moment," said Kentucky Jones, "I can't tell you exactly what happened then; but I can tell you something different, of a very curious interest. On the wall of this house used to be a chromo—an enlarged snapshot—of a man sitting on a horse. You'd look across the room at that little picture, and you'd say to yourself, 'Why, Campo has hung up a lens study of Bob Elliot.' Then maybe you'd look closer; and you'd see it wasn't Bob Elliot at all—but a representation of John Mason."

Sheriff Hopper said, "You mean—you're saying—"

"Bob Elliot knew that sometimes, sitting his horse in a certain way and at a certain distance, he and John Mason looked strangely alike; and Campo had promised to kill Elliot that day. Elliot knew that Campo did not dare take a chance on what a jury might make out of that."

"You're suggesting that Campo Ragland killed Mason by mistake, taking him for Elliot?"

"I'm suggesting that it could be made to look that way; and that Elliot was able to hold that over Campo—and that that was why Elliot dared swamp the Bar Hook range."

"You mean that he ran a bluff that he could bring Ragland to trial for the murder of Mason?"

"You can call it a bluff," said Kentucky Jones, looking at Bob Elliot, "or you could call it a kind of silent black-mail, if you want."

Bob Elliot jerked forward in his chair as if he would come to his feet. "Why, damn your eyes," he said, "if you think I'm going to sit here and take—"

"You'll sit there," Kentucky Jones said coolly, "and you'll take it, and you'll like it. I didn't send for you. You horned in here of your own accord, as I knew you would. But now that you're here, I've only begun."

Elliot exploded, "I'll be damned if—"

"You'll take it," Kentucky repeated. "You'll take it because you're yellow, clear down to the roots. And you haven't forgotten the night I knocked you kicking and squalling, in the sheriff's office at Waterman."

Bob Elliot's face went white, and his eyes took on a squinting slant. His lower lip dropped loose away from his teeth. "Why, you—"

"Yellow," Kentucky repeated, "clear down to the roots."

An inarticulate blasphemy strangled in Elliot's throat. Sheriff Floyd Hopper made a clutch at Elliot's belt, but missed his hold, as Elliot sprang at Kentucky Jones like a quirted horse.

Kentucky Jones hunched low, then straightened out the whole length of his body behind his left hand. There was a ringing crack, as if a bone had broken, and an instant's confused tangle. Then Bob Elliot was lying on his back, breathing hoarsely, staring at the ceiling with blank eyes; and Kentucky Jones stood over him, nursing his left hand in his right.

Hopper said in a low exasperated voice, "You baited him into that, Jones!"

"I was counting on his temper," Kentucky said. "Lord, I thought it would never break!"

Hopper's voice rose angrily. "If you got me out here to

make fools of us all—"

"Shut up," Kentucky snapped at him, "we've got work to do. I—"

"You've talked all around and about, and over the bush," Hopper said bitterly. "And you end up with nothing more to the point than a cheap brawl. You've wasted enough words to—"

"Not one single word," Kentucky contradicted him. "I had to go all over all that so that you would understand what is going to happen—what I hope is going to happen now. Campo! Hold this range hog here when he comes to—put a gun on him if you need to."

"All right."

Jones caught Hopper's arm and dragged the sheriff after him to the door.

"What are you going to do? You've got the case worse scattered out now than—"

"Then we'll try to tie it together again. Here's where we tackle Bill McCord. It's the turn, it's the break, you hear me? I've got to run a bluff. Are you backing me or not?"

"I'm backing you."

"Give me the gun that killed Sanders."

Floyd Hopper obeyed, and Kentucky Jones stuck it in his waistband. "Come on!"

## CHAPTER NINETEEN

Three pairs of eyes turned upon Kentucky Jones and Floyd Hopper as they came into the kitchen. In the room from which they had come, all four men had been armed; and so accustomed had they become to the sagging gun belts as standard equipment in the last few days that here it was Ted Baylor and Bill McCord, who were unarmed, who looked unusual and conspicuous now. Floyd Hopper was flushed and sharp-eyed; but though it was to Hopper the eyes of the three waiting men turned, it was Kentucky Jones who spoke, his face as unpleasantly cold and ugly as ice on broken rock.

He showed Bill McCord the gun that had killed Sanders—the gun that had been in Sanders' hand as Lee Bishop found him dead.

"I don't suppose," he said to McCord, "you ever saw this gun before?"

Bill McCord seemed to consider for a long moment. "Maybe I have," he said at last; "and maybe I haven't."

"Would you care to say where it was when you saw it last?"

A humorless grin twisted one side of McCord's face. "You go to hell," he answered.

Kentucky Jones eyed him sorrowfully. "Is that final?"

"You bet your life it's final!"

"I'm sorry for this," Kentucky said. "I swear to heaven, I believe there's going to be an injustice done. I was afraid of this! But this McCord is a man who means what he says, Floyd; if he won't talk he won't talk. I guess there's nothing to do but follow up what Elliot says—don't it look that way to you?"

Floyd Hopper had no more idea of what Jones was talking about than did McCord. But he was a poker player, and a good one; and he had been in office for a long time. "It sure looks that way," he said.

Kentucky Jones said, "You're under arrest, McCord."

For a moment no one spoke. A hard gleam came into Bill McCord's eyes; his hands, which had been rolling a cigarette, stopped and held perfectly motionless, steady as a rock. "Who says so?" he demanded at last.

Once more the sheriff, completely in the dark as he was, backed Kentucky's play gamely. "I say so," he told McCord.

"Personally," said Kentucky, "I don't think you're guilty, Bill. I'll admit I was kind of hoping that we had closed in on bigger game. Still, I suppose we ought to be glad that we can hang this thing on anybody at all. I guess we better tell you that anything you say will be used against you, McCord."

Bill McCord spat into the wood box. "What am I charged with?" he demanded.

"The murder of Lee Bishop," said Kentucky.

McCord's face hardened, but he went back to the making of his cigarette. "In the first place," he said, "I wasn't anywhere near it. And in the second place it wasn't no murder. Lee Bishop was killed in a fair stand-up fight."

"That lie is plumb useless," said Kentucky contemptuously, "because I was with Lee Bishop when he was killed. Bishop was knocked out of the saddle with a rifle shot, by a man hidden in the rocks three hundred yards away, and the slug that killed him was poured into him after he was down and helpless, and I was carrying him to cover. And my story is proved by the nature of Bishop's wounds. Fair fight, hell! That's murder—you hear me?"

McCord stared at Jones, his face immobile. At last he shook his head, puzzled. "I take all that to be free-hand lying. If you was with Bishop, you'd know that I wasn't there."

"He was shot from cover, I told you," Kentucky said. "I didn't see his killer. I could never have named you as the man—if Bob Elliot hadn't lost his guts."

"Elliot? Him lose his guts?" McCord repeated incredulously. "That's a hot one!"

Kentucky Jones shrugged. "I heard different," he said significantly. "McCord, if you've got anything to say for yourself you sure better talk. Unless you can bring new evidence into this, you've got no more chance than a one-legged man at a pants-kicking. I tell you, Elliot's gone out from under you, you fool!"

Bill McCord stared again, hesitated. Then he laughed shortly. "That's a lie," he decided. "That's a lie from the ground up! Neither me nor Elliot had anything to do with any of this."

"So be it," said Kentucky. "Floyd, bring in Elliot. Or, here—I'll bring him myself." He flashed a malignant grin at McCord, and went out.

Behind him Hopper said to his deputy, "Watch this guy, Willie!" He followed Kentucky Jones.

Kentucky and the sheriff paused for a whispered conference beyond the door.

"By God, Jones," said the sheriff, "I believe that guy knows something."

"Of course he knows something," Kentucky said irritably.

"But he got through the loop on you," Hopper said. "He's too cool and tough to stampede. You've played your ace, and never took a trick. What are you going to do now?"

"Lead the jack," said Kentucky, unperturbed. As he moved on to the room where Campo was holding Bob Elliot he no longer believed that he could lose. He was humming a familiar song:

*"You jack o' diamonds, I knowed you of old—*
*Knowed you of old, baby mine, long ago . . ."*

A dissension was beginning in the little room where Campo was presiding over the now conscious Elliot. Jean and Campo did not appear to have moved; but the boss of the 88 was sitting up in a chair. He leaned forward, his hands gripping the arms, and glowered at Ragland with eyes that seemed not quite able to focus accurately. "Put down that gun," he was saying. "There's no damn—" He checked as Kentucky and the sheriff appeared.

"Tell him," Kentucky whispered sidelong to Hopper, "he's under arrest."

"You're under arrest, Elliot," said the sheriff.

"Tell him," Kentucky prompted, " 'McCord has spilled the beans.' "

"McCord has spilled the beans," the sheriff repeated to

Elliot with convincing emphasis.

Bob Elliot stared at them vaguely for a full quarter of a minute. "I don't know what you're talking about," he said finally.

Kentucky nudged Hopper, but this time the sheriff did not wait for his whispered instructions. For the first time, Hopper seemed ready to go forward under his own power. "You're charged with murder, Elliot," he said. "McCord has told it all."

Elliot stared at the sheriff for a long moment more. "I'll talk to McCord," he said at last, his voice harsh. "Let me talk to McCord."

"I should say not," said the sheriff.

"I should say yes," said Kentucky Jones. "McCord's in the kitchen, Elliot. Just step this way." He pushed the sheriff ahead of him. Bob Elliot rose, swayed for a moment uncertainly, and followed as they returned to the kitchen. Campo trailed along; but Jean stayed where she was.

"Here's your friend, McCord," said Kentucky. "Look him over—and ask yourself what you've been depending on, all this time."

In the doorway Bob Elliot stood, swaying on his legs like a drunken man. The muscles about his mouth twitched, and his eyes were red in a bloodless face.

Looking at the boss of the 88, Bill McCord's jaw sagged. A moment before, McCord had perhaps believed that he knew Bob Elliot; but no one, looking at Elliot now, could say that this was the same man he had known. Elliot might have been sick, or he might have been insane; certainly he bore no resemblance to a man who could be expected to stand firm and steady in a pinch. For the first time Bill McCord was shaken.

"Look each other over," said Kentucky Jones. "A fine pair to draw to—or to build a hanging around."

Bill McCord cried out, "Bob, what the hell you been telling these bastards?"

"What the devil you talking about?" said Elliot "I—"

Kentucky Jones offered Elliot the butt of the gun that had killed Sanders. "Here's your gun, Elliot. They've matched it with the bullets that killed Zack."

A light flared up in Bob Elliot's eyes and he turned on Bill McCord. "If McCord says this is my gun," he exploded, "he lies."

"Ask Ted Baylor," Kentucky said. "Ted, tell the gentlemen where you last saw this gun—after you won it at craps from Joe St. Marie."

Ted Baylor glanced at the gun again, and he hesitated. Kentucky Jones waited, balanced in suspense. He believed that one of the two—McCord or Elliot—would break under the one last straw that Baylor might perhaps provide. But he had not talked to Ted Baylor—had found no chance to talk to him—and he did not know what this man would say.

"I guess you can remember when I saw this gun last, yourself, Bob," said Ted Baylor at last.

"You're crazy," said Elliot.

"I won that gun from Joe St. Marie, in a crap game, one night last fall," Ted Baylor said; "but I didn't have it an hour before I sold it to you, Bob, for two dollars and a half, and the band for a hat."

Bob Elliot said savagely, "You were so damn drunk

that night you don't remember what you did!"

"So that's what you relied on?" said Kentucky Jones. "You thought Baylor was so drunk that the gun could never be traced?"

"I never saw that gun before in my life," said Elliot.

"It was a good idea of yours," said Kentucky, "to throw Bill McCord to the wolves. And it worked good enough so that we'll hang McCord all right; but—"

Bill McCord took a step toward Elliot, his face contorted. "You dirty sneak! So that's your game, is it?" He swung crazily upon Sheriff Hopper. "He's lied to you," he almost shouted. "He's lied to you like he lied to me! I knew he was crazy to get Bishop killed, and I tried to pick a fight with Bishop for that reason. But it never went through. He told me he killed Bishop himself in fair fight. If I'd known he laid for him on the rim and plugged him with a rifle, without fight, I'd have walked out on him!"

Bob Elliot's voice rose violently. "You fool, will you shut your damn mouth before—"

"I suppose," said Kentucky to Bill McCord, "you didn't even know that Bob Elliot killed Mason."

"No, I never—"

"What did you suppose he wanted Bishop killed for? You didn't know he hired you to kill Bishop because Bishop saw him at the Bar Hook the day Mason died?"

Bob Elliot began, "Bill, don't you let these—"

"You lousy streak of yellow," Bill McCord snarled at him, "I see it now! I don't wonder you disown your damn gun! If I'd known when you killed Lee Bishop that you lay off and plugged him with a rifle—"

"It's a damn lie!" said Bob Elliot again.

"Is it?" McCord snarled at him. "I suppose it's a lie that you strapped on that gun and rode after Mason, that day when he laughed in your face—"

"By God, McCord—" Elliot shouted.

"Put it off on me, will you?" McCord shouted back at him. "I thought maybe you killed Mason, when you told me you knew he was killed with Campo's rifle. Why, you dirty side-winder—"

Bob Elliot's voice broke into something almost like a squeal. "You damned—" Suddenly he turned, lurched crazily at the door behind him, and was gone from the room.

Willie Helmar cried, "Shall I get him? Shall I get him?"

"McCord," roared Sheriff Hopper, "is this true?"

"Sure, it's true!" McCord frothed. "I can see it now— and I can prove it on him every step of the way! Hang me in his place, will he? Why, that—"

Suddenly Bill McCord's face changed as if it had been struck with a whip. He whirled like a cat, snatched at the holstered gun of Willie Helmar; and though Helmar seized McCord's arm as the gun came out, McCord wrenched free. In that instant Jean, in the next room, screamed, "Kentucky, look out!" And Bob Elliot's first shot spoke from the door.

The next moment was one of those which witnesses afterward describe conflictingly, so that it is difficult to know the truth.

Kentucky Jones shouted, "Jean, get out of line!" and though he fired in the direction of Bob Elliot, he seemed to fire at the floor. Elliot dropped to one knee. Kentucky instantly fired again, his second shot smashing Bill McCord's gun wrist, so that McCord was spun half about. Almost in accord with Kentucky's second shot Bob Elliot fired again. Kentucky Jones stepped sideways as he once more fired on Bob Elliot. This time Bob Elliot went forward onto his face; and his gun, slamming from his relaxed hand, skidded half way across the floor toward Kentucky Jones. Then gun and man lay still, and the room was still, heavy with the peculiar unforgettable smell of smokeless powder. . . .

"Kentucky," said Sheriff Hopper, "what's happened here?"

The debris had been cleared away, by now. Elliot, not as seriously hit as, under the circumstances, he might himself have wished, was officially in custody, as was Bill McCord; and Floyd Hopper was four miles up in the air.

"You don't need to watch Bill McCord so close," Kentucky said; "he's ready to tell you enough to convict Elliot before any Wolf Bench jury, without any more trouble. Your case was clinched the minute you found out that Sanders was killed with the gun that was found in his hand. It's been plain all along that Sanders was killed because he witnessed the killing of Mason; and you've heard McCord identify the gun that killed Sanders."

"But look here," Hopper insisted. "Up to the time that you got Elliot and McCord all crossed up, you hadn't even talked to Ted Baylor."

"I didn't have time to get hold of him," Kentucky

explained, "in the little time after I found out from St. Marie that the gun had passed through Baylor's hands. But then that wasn't necessary, hardly. Elliot had to have full information before he dared to flood the Bar Hook range. And he couldn't have got all those cattle on the move as quick as he did unless he had started working them the next morning after Mason was killed. He could hardly have got such full information so quick—unless he had killed Mason himself."

"But you didn't know how many hands that gun passed through besides Ted Baylor's. Ted Baylor might have passed it on to almost anybody. You couldn't count on him to name the gun as Elliot's gun."

"Sure not. But that didn't matter. It's McCord's identification that counts. Of course, it might have been that that gun had wound up at the Bar Hook, and that Elliot walked in and borrowed it, the same as he did Campo's rifle. In that case, of course, there wouldn't have been any tangible evidence against Elliot, and we'd have lost out all around. But I figured that the killer would have shot quick with his own gun, in Zack's case; and then shoved the same gun into Zack's hand. He would have been in a hurry to get out of there about then."

"But how did you know that the gun in Sanders' hand wasn't Zack's own gun? Now there—*that* was the turning point of the whole thing."

"You didn't see that that wasn't Zack's gun?"

"Can I know every gun in the rimrock? How could any man guess it wasn't his?"

"You mean you thought Zack rode all over Wolf Bench carrying that gun in his hand?"

"In his hand? What you driving at?"

"He would have had to carry it in his hand. Sanders had no gun belt," Kentucky reminded him—"he wasn't even wearing boots. And there wasn't a single pocket in his clothes that that gun would go in. . . ."

Within an hour after the showdown which had thrown Elliot into the sheriff's hands, Hopper had forgotten his gratification over the solution in his alarm over the storm which he was sure would follow. Tomorrow word of the charge against Elliot would have swept the rim-rock. Already Floyd Hopper could see himself facing the mobs which he now supposed would wish to take the law into their own hands—mobs made difficult by the unnoisy but peculiarly efficient purposefulness of cowmen who have made up their minds. If the sheriff knew his brush poppers—and he thought he did—unpleasantness was going to come down on him in sheets; and he was already more interested in plans to smuggle Elliot to some far safe confinement than he was in what had already been accomplished.

With only a few hours' margin for the completion of preventive measures the sheriff barged off to Waterman. With him went his brother, Doc Hopper, who had been rushed out meantime to administer first aid; and Bill McCord.

Late afternoon found the Bar Hook locked in that restive, exhausted quiet which follows any kind of explosion. Somewhere in the house Willie Helmar sat watchfully beside the wounded Elliot, who propped himself up in bed and smoked interminably, saying nothing at all. Ted Baylor had left, and Campo had drawn off by himself.

Kentucky Jones sat alone in the big kitchen, slowly drinking coffee that he did not want, and watching, through the smoke of his cigarette, the golden motes that swam in the horizontal sunlight from the west.

He wanted to talk to Jean—knew that he must talk to Jean; and he dreaded it, for he had no remotest notion of what he would be able to say. Now that the war of the 88 upon the Bar Hook was killed at the source, and the death of Mason no longer was a mystery which hung over Campo Ragland, Kentucky Jones found himself comprehending, as if for the first time, the full weight of the burden which Jean had chosen to bear alone.

At one time, he thought, Jean must have believed her father guilty of the murder of Mason. For him she had smothered the evidence, at once concealing her father's supposed involvement and concealing her knowledge from Campo himself. To her Lee Bishop had told a story which he himself did not understand; she had known the exact status of St. Marie and Kentucky Jones, and the truth about the missing rifle and the picture that was gone from its frame. What Kentucky had said was true—that every one had confided in her, and she had confided in none. And through every hour of those days she most certainly had known that she was carrying in her own hands the lives of men who meant more to her than any others in the world.

As Kentucky considered this it seemed to him that he had never witnessed in any man the gameness, the courage, nor the fixed fidelity of purpose of this one slender girl.

He wanted to seek her out now, and tell her that he knew what she had faced; and that the victory was not Sheriff Hopper's, nor his own, but hers, and hers only. And he knew he would have no words to express any part of that. He almost convinced himself this was not the time to try to talk to her; that he should pack out of there, and go to Waterman, and come back some time a long while later.

Then a door closed softly in another part of the house, and he jerked to his feet.

He found her at the stable shed where the saddles were. She had already roped a pony—the same pony with which she had met him early that morning upon the trail—and she was saddling with hurried, unsteady hands.

"Where you going, Jean?"

"What do you care where I'm going?" she said in a small vague voice. "Who gives a whoop? Least of all myself."

He went to his saddle, and took down his rope. She watched him shake out a little cat-loop.

"What—what are you going to do?"

"I thought," he said, "I'd reach me down a horse, and come along."

Her hands dropped the latigo, and she turned to face him. Except that it was daylight now, and the low sun behind her outlined her figure with flame, they stood now almost as they had stood here the night that he had trapped her, after her unexplained rendezvous with Bob Elliot.

"No!" she told him. "No, no! I don't want you to

come. I—I want to be alone—" Her face was white.

"Just as you want, Jean," he answered slowly. "Only—I just thought that you and I had been through too much here, together, to ride two trails now. I don't blame you though, if you hate the hell out of me."

"It isn't that," she said brokenly. "Kentucky, it isn't that. It's myself that I hate the hell out of."

"Why, child, what's the matter?"

Suddenly Jean broke. She sat down in a heap upon a spare saddle, and hid her face in her arms. "I—wish I were dead." The words came to him half smothered, inarticulate.

He dropped to one knee beside her. "Jean! What is it?"

"Lee Bishop—poor Lee—"

Kentucky considered. "Did you love him, Jean?"

For a moment she lifted her face to stare at him. "Did I what? Love him? No. But—oh, dear God, Kentucky—it's my fault he isn't alive today."

"What nonsense is this?" he demanded.

"I killed him, Kentucky; I killed him just as sure as—as if I'd gunned him myself."

"That's the worst bunk I ever heard in my life!"

She shook her head again; her words were muffled and incoherent. "You don't know. You don't know. . . . If only I'd trusted you then! I've trusted you since, Kentucky; I have, I have! I'd put anything in the world in your hands, with never a flicker of a doubt. But then—I thought I had to play it out alone. Everybody trusted me, but I trusted nobody—just as you said. After Lee told me he had seen Mason here the day Mason died—I knew it was Bob Elliot he had seen. And when Elliot began swamping our range I phoned him, and rode out to meet him, and I tried to bluff him out. I told him that Lee had seen him there—that we could turn the case against him if he opened the play. I thought I could hold that over him, and bluff him off. Instead—it only meant Lee's death. Kentucky, Kentucky, it's my fault he's dead. If ever blame could be placed in this world, that blame is on me!"

"Poor child," he said. "Poor child! Jean, I guess Lee didn't tell you it all; but he told me before he died. Didn't Lee tell you that he hailed the man he thought was Mason? He hailed, and waved; the other didn't answer—but it's certain that Elliot knew Lee saw him, because McCord tried to pick a fight with Bishop, *before* you talked to Elliot. Don't you see? The cards were against Lee all the time, and you had nothing to do with it at all."

She lifted her face, and gripped both his arms. "Kentucky—is this true—are you sure—"

"Why, of course, child. I—"

Once more she hid her face, this time weeping unrestrainedly. Kentucky gathered her into his arms. "Whatever else has happened here," he told her, "this thing is true: nobody in the world has ever been as game, and as brave, and as true as you've been, through all this long stampede. There isn't your equal any place, and never has been, you hear me? And not a man of us here, or anywhere, is fit to saddle your bronc."

Presently, as he held her, the shuddering jerk of her breathing subsided, and she was quiet in his arms. "It's been so lonely, so terrible, for so long," she whispered at last. "Hold me tight, Kentucky; don't let me go."

"No," he answered; "not ever any more."

**Center Point Publishing**
600 Brooks Road • PO Box 1
Thorndike ME 04986-0001 USA

(207) 568-3717

US & Canada:
1 800 929-9108

H